WORDS ACROSS TIME

An Illustrated Anthology

by

Windmore Writers and Artists

Windmore Foundation for the Arts

Published by

Windmore Foundation for the Arts
P.O. Box 38
Culpeper, VA 22701
(540) 547-4333
www.windmorefoundation.org

The mission of the Windmore Foundation for the Arts is to promote the visual, literary, and performing arts through awareness, participation, and education.

The views expressed in these materials represent the opinions of the respective authors. Publication of these materials does not constitute an endorsement by Windmore Foundation for the Arts, Inc., of any views expressed herein, and Windmore Foundation for the Arts disclaims any liability arising from any inaccuracy or misstatement.

Cover and text design and composition by Jack Daily
Cover image © Kathleen Willingham
Co-Edited by Caryn Block, Fran Cecere, D.J. Christiano, Jack Daily, Judith Dreyer, Bette Hileman, Dawn Latham, Lisa Pugh, and Bobbie Troy

Copyright © 2012 D.C. Windmore Foundation for the Arts.

All rights reserved by the individual authors and artists. No part of this publication may be reproduced, stored in a retrieval system, or transmitted in any form or by any means electronic, mechanical, photocopying, recording, or otherwise without the prior permission of the publisher.

ISBN-10: 1478387637
ISBN-13: 978-1478387633

Library of Congress Catalog Number: 2012947678

Printed in the United States of America

Table of Contents

PREFACE XII

ACKNOWLEDGMENTS XIII

SIX-SENTENCE STORIES 1

    The Dragon Lord 2
    Caryn Moya Block

    Melody From The Past 2
    Diane Burdette

    The Judge 3
    Judith Dreyer

    Satin Dreams 3
    Fran Cecere

    Righteousness 4
    Bobbie Troy

    Didn't She? 4
    Caryn Moya Block

    Arts and Humanities 5
    Jack Daily

A TRAIN OF THOUGHT 7

    Waterloo Station: As Two Wars End 9
    Lisa Pugh

    Things I Should Have Said 19
    Bobbie Troy

    The Travel Guide 20
    Jennifer Bierhulzen

    30th Street Station 24
    D.C. Ackerly

    Making Change 25
    Cynthia Siira

Old Woman at the Train Depot 32
Ruby E. Pruitt

A Modern Train Station 35
D.J. Christiano

FACES IN STONE 39

Wanderings of Self 41
Bobbie Troy

While Eavesdropping on Two Cherubs 42
Ruby E. Pruitt

Two Cherubs 44
Judith Dreyer

Treasured Faces 47
D.J. Christiano

A Visit With Cherubs 48
Fran Cecere

Twins 50
Jennifer Bierhuizen

Stuck In Stone 51
Caryn Moya Block

A LOOK BACK 53

1992 54
Windmore Writers Anthology

Santa Claus Came in a Barrel 54
Sarah Calvert Hitt

1996 57
Touching the Heart

evening fall 57
Cora DeJarnette Chlebnikow

Our Old Hayloft 58
John Henry

untitled 62
Cora DeJarnette Chlebnikow

unpublished 63
Cora DeJarnette Chlebnikow

2010 64
Images in Ink

Cricket in a Jar 64
Pennie L. Kinsey

Patience 70
Herbert Frisbee

Thoughts 71
MaryAnn Morrison

Fish and Potatoes 73
Bette Hileman

Bare Huntin' 78
Herbert Frisbie

Cab Ride 79
D.C. Ackerly

Unconscious Color 81
Marlee Laws

The Memory Tree 82
Fran Cecere

REFLECTIONS... 85

Pet Adoption 86
Diane Burdette

The Tiger in the Tile 87
Pennie Patterson

The Savior in Cat Alley 92
Bobbie Troy

What Goes Up 93
Fran Cecere

Spinning 97
Jack Daily

Ordinary Hope 98
D.J. Christiano

An Atypical Tuesday 103
Diane Burdette

My Lunch Date in Charlottesville............................. 104
MaryAnn Morrison

A Look Into the Past 108
Caryn Moya Block

The Easter Suit 111
Lois Powell

Miracle Worker.. 115
Gwen Monohan

A Blue Screen Chat 116
Jack Daily

IN HER WORDS.. 117

A Writer's Dream 118
Ruby E. Pruit

The Yard Sale... 119
Lavanda Woodall

Tomorrow Is on Hold 124
Bobbie Troy

Son Leaving for College 125
Martha Orr Conn

Ladies' Man.. 126
Lavanda Woodall

Woman on the Porch 131
Bobbie Troy

Unlikely Fantasy 133
Martha Orr Conn

Second-Story Man 134
Lavanda Woodall

Journaling... 139
Sophi Link

Facing Self-Doubt 141
Bobbie Troy

One Day You Will Do This Too!...................................143
Ruby E. Pruitt

BEYOND REALITY 145

The Guarding Stones...147
Caryn Moya Block

The East Side of Satisfaction 149
jd young

...What Problem? 158
Marlee Laws

A Gift for a Goddess: A Polynesian Snippet................159
Lisa Pugh

The Gift 171
Jack Daily

Weird 174
jd young

In Another Light...179
Jack Daily

Seeing Reality 180
Marlee Laws

AN INVITATION TO PONDER 181

In the Forest 183
Judith Dreyer

Circles and Hands 184
Bobbie Troy

My Mind Is Free...185
Bobbie Troy

Musical Memories 186
Sophi Link

It Exists 188
Pennie Patterson

The Future Storm 189
Pennie Patterson

Absinthe 191
D.C. Ackerly

A Thirty-Percent Chance of Rain 192
Jack Daily

Too Many Secrets 193
jd young

Break Your Silent Thoughts 195
Jack Daily

A Change in Weather 195
Jack Daily

Angel of . . . What? 197
Martha Orr Conn

Unfinished Statements 198
Marlee Laws

Dressed for Work 199
Bobbie Troy

Snow 200
Caryn Moya Block

Star Power 202
Gwen Monohan

Direction is Everything 203
Jack Daily

Looking Within 204
MaryAnn Morrison

In Quiet Shadows 205
Jack Daily

A Song in Celebration of Soaring 206
Pennie L. Kinsey

Softball Slugger 209
Diane Burdette

Random Thoughts on Life 212
Bobbie Troy

THE SANDS OF TIME 213

In Childhood 215
Diane Burdette

Growing Up 216
MaryAnn Morrison

Confidence 217
Bobbie Troy

Before I Could Fly 219
Judith Dreyer

A Change of Heart 220
Nancy Scott

Moments Passed 221
jd young

In Three Minutes 222
Jack Daily

Change the Record, Will You 223
Jack Daily

Life of Tides 226
Sophi Link

A Glow From Within 229
Diane Burdette

Surviving Auschwitz 231
Bobbie Troy

Bedtime 232
Nancy Scott

No More Sad Songs 233
Jack Daily

The Old Age Repository 234
Bobbie Troy

LOVE'S SPELL 237

Isabelle's Cowboy 239
Caryn Moya Block

The Cowboy 240
Jan Settle

He Would Wait 242
Judith Dreyer

Merry Christmas, My Love 246
Bobbie Troy

Pretense...247
Bobbie Troy

An Unexpected Pleasure...249
Caryn Moya Block

Unrequited 254
Marlee Laws

Destiny 255
jd young

Relative Madness 256
Sophi Link

Finding Love Again 257
Judith Dreyer

Pearl 259
Pennie L. Kinsey

My Love... 261
jd young

That Day 263
Jack Daily

Plowed Under..264
Gwen Monohan

We'll Meet When It's Right 265
Judith Dreyer

FEEDING THE CREATIVE FIRES 267

Tails From the Sea 269
D.J. Christiano

Dear Diane 275
Bobbie Troy

Advice To My Newly Married Son 276
Martha Orr Conn

The Art of Pasta 277
Jack Daily

A Family Favorite 278
Diane Burdette

Open Some More Wine 279
Fran Cecere

So Much Ado 283
Jack Daily

ON THE EDGE 285

It's A Miracle 286
Fran Cecere

Samantha 292
Bobbie Troy

Striptease Variation 293
Marlee Laws

I Want To Be Human 294
Pennie Patterson

Ba Da Bang! 296
Jack Daily

BIOGRAPHIES 299

Preface

This 2012 anthology, *Words Across Time*, is a celebration of twenty years of creative writing by members of the Windmore Foundation for the Arts. For months the writers from Pen-to-Paper submitted their poems, stories, and essays to the anthology committee. It was difficult to select from such amazing talent. The anthology team chose the submissions that touched us by making us think, laugh, or cry.

To complete the journey through time, selections from three other Windmore anthologies were used to represent previous years. Those books are: *Windmore Writers' Anthology*, 1992; *Touching the Heart*, 1996; and *Images in Ink*, 2010. The authors from those anthologies are pleased that their work is still recognized as relevant.

The artists of Windmore contributed beautiful, original art work inspired by stories in the book. Literature and art together add charm to this publication.

If you are interested in learning more about Pen-to-Paper or would like to join our local group, please send an e-mail to pentopaper@windmorefoundation.org.

Fran Cecere
Chairperson of the Anthology Committee

Acknowledgments

The Anthology Committee would like to thank the writers who submitted their poems and stories to the anthology. The project team listed alphabetically consisted of Caryn Block, Fran Cecere, D.J. Christiano, Jack Daily, Judith Dreyer, Bette Hileman, Dawn Latham, Lisa Pugh, and Bobbie Troy. Many members of the team put in countless hours reading, editing, and making suggestions for changes to the submissions. Also, we appreciate those members who read the early anthologies and helped select the materials to be used in this twenty-year history of creative writing.

We extend our thanks to the Windmore Artist Group for their contributions. The group's original artwork was completed cheerfully and enthusiastically. Jack Daily used his photography and computer skills to complete the layout of the book. His commitment to this anthology was invaluable. We owe a debt of gratitude to Windmore Foundation for the Arts for continuing to support Pen-to-Paper in all its endeavors, especially the publication of this anthology.

We also would like to thank our families who tolerated our time away from home and hours of reading while at home. Without the support of our loved ones, this book would never have made it to press.

All of the proceeds from this book will be contributed to Windmore Foundation for the Arts so that it can continue to support the arts in our Culpeper community.

Six-Sentence Stories

Want a challenging writing prompt? Write a story explaining the plot, characters, setting, and conflict. Now do all of that in just six sentences.

The Dragon Lord
Caryn Moya Block

He had said he would come for her, and today was the day. The rift between dimensions parted, and he was standing before her. Her soul and heart cried out and reached for him, but her mind resisted. As he swept her into his arms, gone was the grandmother she had become, and instead was the young woman who always resided in her soul. Holding her close to his chest, he turned to carry her back to the other side. As they stepped through the portal, she wondered if this was the beginning of a new life or a descent into old age and madness.

Melody From The Past
Diane Burdette

Isn't it funny how a song can evoke a memory? As the music plays, I think about that special summer. Suddenly, I'm reunited with loved ones in a Scottish pub. I remember exploring castles, hillsides, and quaint, old villages. And at summer's end, our neighbors gathered, and we celebrated with birthday cake and lemon beer. All too soon the song is ending, but for me, images of 1969 still linger.

The Judge
Judith Dreyer

She slammed the book closed, not caring where it fell or what it smashed. Feeling stumped, puzzled, and betrayed, she paced around the chamber. His books lined the walls framed in bookshelves of rich polished cherry that had impressed her not long ago. His robe lay tossed to the floor like black rotted flesh, though the smell came from fear. Truth and justice were not on the scales today and never had been. He was bought and left her on the other side of justice where shadows rob your grave.

Satin Dreams
Fran Cecere

On her wedding day, the shapely beautiful girl looked exquisite in her ivory-colored satin gown. She married a tall, smart, handsome man just as she had predicted she would. He was born to a poor family but struggled to become a lawyer, judge, and highly respected man. She lived the perfect life of a rich woman who was the mother of four gifted children. Those of us still in the old neighborhood envied her storybook lifestyle. Then, one day she violently shredded her wedding dress, ran off with the garbage man, and was never seen again.

Righteousness
Bobbie Troy

Righteousness exuded from his pores as he stood in the pulpit giving the Sunday sermon. The congregation found it strange that he chose the same commandment as last month: Thou Shalt Not Commit Adultery. Returning home, he entered his wife's bedroom quietly. She looked at her husband of thirty years with curious eyes. Her useless right arm was buried among the tangle of sheets.

"I'll fetch the nurse," he said, as he bent over to kiss her forehead gently, perhaps to help assuage his guilt.

Originally published May 10, 2011 in the Journal of Microliterature:
http://www.microliterature.org/?s=bobbie+troy.t.

Didn't She?
Caryn Moya Block

Didn't she hear the rumors of the strange killings?
Didn't she find the house on the hill looming and frightening?
Didn't she wonder why the front door was unlocked?
Didn't she see his shadow on the wall?
Didn't she hear his heavy breathing?
Didn't she see the light glinting off the knife?

Arts and Humanities

Jack Daily

I was a normal child who went to public school and made average grades, mostly *C*'s, a few *B*'s, the uncommon *A*, and a big fat *F* in a winter-term elective in Arts and Humanities. In my first class Miss Ryder had fervently preached: "Without art and religion we are just another animal." But I really liked animals—more than most people I had met. I spent the rest of that class daydreaming about my Yorkies Yin and Yang; my chubby cat Carlos; and the hamsters Larry, Joe, and Moe. As the bell rang, I scribbled my angry thoughts into the otherwise blank notebook, handed it to Miss Ryder on the way out, and marched to the principal's office for sentencing.

That summer, I earned a *B* in Arts and Humanities make-up, Miss Ryder rescued a dog from the animal shelter, and Carlos ate Moe without remorse.

A Train of Thought

Inspired by an Art Deco train station in Philadelphia, these stories transport you to times past and into the future with unforgettable characters and circumstances. Now boarding...

Photograph: © Jack Daily

Waterloo Station: As Two Wars End
Lisa Pugh

December 1918

Army Captain Sir Andrew Smythe rolled his wheelchair into Waterloo Station. It was four years since he'd been in London, and so little had changed. So much had changed. The marble floor was the same. The room was lit by electric lamps. There were the same wood benches, the same kiosks announcing the comings and goings of trains and people.

To him, it was the people who had altered the most. A more sober atmosphere permeated the foyer. There were fewer smiles, more frowns, and more people sitting alone. Then again, perhaps he had changed. Perhaps this time, he noticed those whom his naive, youthful eyes had overlooked before.

There were plenty of people like him among the crowd. So many veterans of the Great War filled his vision—the walking wounded, the walking dead. They had arms missing, legs missing, fingers or vision gone. They were the crippled, the lame, the emotionally destroyed, all surrounded and avoided by the whole and hale.

"I say! If it isn't old Stinky Smythe! Hello, Stinker!" A voice called from his right, from the normal side of his face.

Sir Andrew closed his eyes. Someone from his past—from before the rats, bombs, mud, and gas—had recognized him. This was someone from his Eton days . . . the last person he wanted to see.

He didn't want any of his old friends to see him like this; a few fingers short, voice and half a face ravaged by gas, nothing below the knees. Though they'd never know it, not much to speak of between the legs either. All thanks to Kitchener's Army and Field Marshall Sir Douglas Haig . . . and about 12 million Germans, of course.

"Stinky?" The voice was closer now. "Dear old Stinker, it's me, George Marshall!"

Why him? Of all the school fellows he had to meet, why did it have to be "Marshy" Marshall? The man couldn't get into the Royal Military College at Sandhurst, even with all his connections. Of course, when the war came, those self-same connections kept him miles away from any fighting.

The man was a lazy cretin and had been as a schoolboy at Eton. A master at shirking work, he always found some bright, charity underclassman to do his papers for him. The Yanks say, "Money talks," and he made it speak loud and clear.

With a sigh, the Captain turned his chair around. George skidded to a halt. As the young man gaped at his wounded classmate, Smythe took the opportunity to study him. Marshall looked well-fed and perfectly groomed. The rationing and hardships that most of the British population faced due to U-Boats prowling the trade routes apparently hadn't affected his corner of the world. The man looked disgustingly prosperous, in fact.

Sir Andrew couldn't remember if George's family held stocks in the munitions industry. It made him sick to think that, while he and just about every other healthy male risked their lives and minds in the trenches, this waste of flesh was growing rich safe at home.

"I say!" George exclaimed with open horror. "I'd heard you were wounded, but I never imagined . . . your face . . . your legs!"

"Yes," Smythe rasped, his voice as ragged and scarred as his countenance, "it's amazing what mustard gas and Boche artillery can do."

"Your voice too?" George shook his head, clucking his tongue. "A real tragedy! And you were the most handsome boy in school, or so all the girls at the pub said."

"It happened to a lot of us." The Captain shrugged, not wanting to think about it too much.

Marshall took a deep breath and shook off his momentary sympathy. "Ah well! All for King and Country, what? I'm sure you gave the Huns a dashed good thrashing in return. Just to show them what we British are made of, eh, old chap?"

With a smile that didn't quite reach his eyes, Andrew replied, "I'm sure I fulfilled my quota." He tried to ignore the faces that floated into his mind; young boys in gray uniforms who died in agony . . . lying in No-Man's Land with their British counterparts dead on top of them.

"What? Oh, quite! Yes, very droll."

"It was great to see you, dear Marshy," Andrew lied politely, trying to end this farce of a conversation. "I'm sure you have plenty of other things to do."

"Yes, of course! Busy, busy, busy, that's me!" George seemed relieved to have been given a way to exit gracefully. In the act of leaving, he stopped and turned back. "You know, I think you should come to dinner sometime. Sammy would love to see you."

"Sammy?"

"Yes, Samantha Marshall, *née* Higgins, my wife. You remember her, of the Chester Higginses. She went to that girl's academy up the road from Eton."

"Ah, yes!" Yes, he remembered Samantha; all flawless skin, blue eyes, and hair the color of ripened wheat. How he used to dream of running his hands through that lovely harvest of hair! "I didn't know you had married her. Congratulations."

"Thank you, Stinky. We had our first child not quite a year ago now. Little Georgie's brilliant, just like his mother. We're to have another soon. If we have another boy, we've agreed to name him Marcus, after Sammy's grandfather. Just hope the poor little blighter doesn't look like that old man. A more dour and humorless sort you've never met." George dug in his pocket and drew out a small gold case. "Here's my card. Just give me a call once you're settled, and we can arrange a nice visit. I'm sure Samantha would love to greet one of the heroes of the hour."

"Thank you, Marshy. I'll think about it." He took the ivory-colored card. They said their farewells, and Marshall hurried off in the direction of the platform.

Sir Andrew gazed at the small piece of pasteboard in his hand. George's name, family manor address and phone number were printed in an elaborate script.

With a sigh, Andrew tossed the expensive calling card into the rubbish bin. He was not going to the house of such a bounder. And he certainly was not going to let Samantha Marshall, née Higgins, see him as he was. Better she remember the strong handsome man he had been, rather than the disfigured cripple he had become.

Andrew was sure George wouldn't mind not receiving a call. He'd probably be relieved. Hell, he'd probably forgotten meeting his old schoolmate already. George Marshall had a great mind for forgetting distasteful or disturbing things.

§§§

Twenty-seven years later, 1945

Eye patch firmly in place, Major Sir Roger Smythe hobbled off the train and into the station's foyer. The crowd flowed around him as he stopped and inhaled deeply. The obnoxious pong of cigarettes, car exhaust and smog hit his nostrils. At that moment, a field of flowers in springtime could not have smelled sweeter to him. London. Home.

His good eye took in his surroundings. Old Waterloo—with its wooden benches, marble floor, large windows and Art Deco lighting—welcomed him like an old friend. As with the rest of the capital, Waterloo Station was a little worse for wear. Bombs and rockets had been a near-daily occurrence during the last years of the war. Scorch marks on the walls, holes in the ceiling, cracks in the marble, and broken masonry piled on the floor told of many near-misses and a few direct hits.

Yet, the atmosphere of the place and the people was totally different than it had been when he left for Africa, and later the Continent. The oppressive fear and tension were gone. People were relieved, almost content. They were eager to put this lovely city back together, to rebuild a nation brought so close to disaster.

He could breathe again. The joy of being back in Old Blighty was beyond measure. Six years away, with only two short trips back to retool and get ready for a new theater of operations, had seemed like several eternities.

Looking about him, he remembered how his Uncle Andrew had described his return from the Great War. The difference would have shocked the old man, if he had seen the camaraderie and respect shown to the returning soldiers of this war. The wounded weren't avoided; they were welcomed. They were thanked. They were aided.

They weren't treated as diseased, nor as bitter reminders of the millions not returning. Seeing the many wounded as a burden may come later, but for now they were heroes of a grateful nation. They were saviors of King and Country in a more real, tangible way than the veterans of the Great War had been.

The average British subject understood the importance of the fight. He knew his way of life had been directly threatened and would have been destroyed but for these men. The civilian population had been through a different hell, but they had had a taste of war they'd never forget.

The enemy hadn't been some vague menace, some disturbing monster in the European closet, nor a specter haunting the Continent. He had come knocking at their very doorstep. He had dropped fire and death from the skies onto their very homes, burning many landmarks of this proud land. The British people had experienced the ravages of war firsthand. They did not have to rely on newsreels, newspapers or propaganda to understand the devastation. It was here.

Oddly, knowing those around him understood some of the horrors of war made his return less bitter-sweet than it might have been.

"Roger?" a wavering voice called. "Roger Smythe?"

Oh God! Marcus Marshall! Of all the people to recognize him, he had to be spotted by that funk-hole rat! As his father had before him, he had avoided active service on the front lines. His excuse was some invented malady of the heart . . . or was it the pancreas? It was the same justification given for why he was unable to do athletics or indeed anything strenuous at Eton, such as required chores.

The last person Roger wanted to speak to was that cowardly blighter. However, the voice indicated the man, if he could be called that, was too close to ignore. Smythe couldn't pretend not to hear him. With a sigh, he turned to his old classmate.

The army officer froze. The gentleman approaching him was thin, drawn, and hunched, with thick glasses and a noticeable limp. A decoration hung from the left breast of his jacket. The Major recognized it as the George Medal, a new award given to civilians for significant bravery or extreme valor.

The smile on the young man's face was uneasy, almost embarrassed. When Marshall put out his left hand, the soldier became aware that the right arm shoved in Marcus's jacket pocket wasn't functioning.

Shocked, Smythe put out his left hand. "Marcus! I didn't expect to see anyone I knew."

Words Across Time

"Sorry to be so rude," Marcus explained in that same weak, halting way. "I'd never shake with the left, but the blasted right doesn't work anymore."

"I understand. No problem," the Major replied, regaining his composure. Looking at his schoolmate's pale face and unsteady gait, he was quickly reevaluating his opinion of Marcus's "phantom illness."

"It's been a long time."

"Yes, it has. How's the old family doing then?" Roger forced the polite question.

Marcus dropped his eyes for a moment. "Gone."

"Gone? All of them?"

"I'm afraid so. My mother succumbed to her consumption shortly before the war. Had you heard?"

Smythe had, but he had quickly forgotten it. The news had struck him with nothing more than general sympathy, as if finding out about a stranger's death.

"Pater was in Coventry, training the Home Guard there, when Jerry leveled the town. Margaret was a WAAF. She worked at a radar installation on the coast. Stutkas hit her barracks three years back."

"And Georgie?" George Marshall the second, several years their senior, had been the only member of the family Roger could tolerate in large quantities. The eldest sibling, George had been extremely bright, friendly, and humorous.

"You remember how wonderful he was at mathematics? He was sent as a turret gunner in the Lancasters. Many mathematicians were, since they could calculate quickly in their head the declensions and angles needed to shoot moving planes accurately." Marcus sighed. "The Luftwaffe got him over Hamburg."

"I'm sorry, Marcus." Roger knew Georgie had been Marcus's hero. A natural athlete, the older brother had excelled at sports and displayed enormous strength. He could do anything, and out-think anyone. More importantly, George had defended his younger brother from bullies at school and had never made him feel useless or worthless because the smaller boy couldn't equal his physical accomplishments.

The young man shrugged. "It's the war. I'm not inept in math and logic myself, but my health would never tolerate those altitudes. I became a part of the Bletchley Park crowd and worked at code breaking. All very hush-hush."

"Seems a fairly safe job, barring spies. Your arm and leg . . ."

"A stray V-2 hit my flat in town. If that old wobbly wardrobe hadn't fallen on me, I would have lost more than a operational wing and my smooth walk. As it is, helping other residents get out while wounded got me this nice decoration." Despite his light-hearted tone, he touched his George Medal with pride and reverence.

Listening to the off-handed way Marcus spoke, without self-pity or bitterness, Roger found himself admiring his old schoolfellow. That was something he never thought he'd feel.

"I'm sorry, Marcus."

"Thanks, Roger. Coming from you, with the war you probably had, that means a lot." The code breaker gave a sad smile. "I know what people at school thought of me, that I was a shirker and a bounder. Like father like son, right? But I'd like to think that my work at Bletchley contributed in some small way to defeating the Nazis. It wasn't quite El Alamain or the Rhine, but perhaps it was something."

Roger started with surprise. Obviously, Marcus had followed his career carefully, when he had barely given him a second thought. He suddenly remembered that Marcus had watched with a kind of sad envy while his classmates played sports and games. He had tried to help with the chores, carrying the trash bins out and such, but always had to stop and beg off, panting. The other students had scoffed at him, and called him a weakling and a ninny. So had Roger. Seeing his fellow Etonian now, the Major felt that hadn't been "his finest hour."

Marcus glanced briefly, even casually, at the Major's cane and eyepatch. "I see the war didn't treat you any better than it did me. I suppose that shouldn't be surprising. So few have come out of this mess completely whole." There was no disgust or overt sympathy in his voice, merely an observation of reality.

"A sniper got my leg during a firefight outside of Bonn. My eye was my own fault—flash burn from an explosion. Forgot to keep my head down around mortars."

Marcus smiled slightly. "I see. Is any of it permanent?"

"Don't know yet. My leg will heal, I suppose, but it will never be as strong as it was. Too much damage to the bone, you see. I will probably lose some sight in the eye. The patch protects it from dust and shields the nerves from light. Even the slightest glow feels like a thousand needles in my brain at the moment. It also hides some of the scarring. If the eye recovers, I may be able to lose this accessory."

"Seems the war didn't do either of us any favors." Marcus pointed toward a small sandwich shop nestled in a corner of the lobby. "Care for some coffee or tea? I'll pay."

Roger blinked in shock. "They have coffee and tea here?"

"Well some God-awful equivalent anyway. Old Prime Minister Attlee says we shouldn't expect to find our usual creature comforts any time soon. Until then, we have warm water that passes as tea, and turpentine which they call coffee."

"Ah! Sounds like army rations!" Roger grinned. "Lead the way. It will be nice to have a cuppa without fearing bullets or bombs."

"Yes, indeed! Still haven't gotten used to passing an entire day and night without those bloody air-raid sirens. The quiet is . . . odd, unsettling."

Major Smythe understood. The sudden silence when peace was declared had been deafening. "Come on. Let's get tea."

The two classmates strode to the cafe, more friendly at that moment than they'd ever been at school.

Things I Should Have Said
Bobbie Troy

I should have said
that your tears
were like antique pearls
gracing porcelain cheeks

I should have said
that I would take those pearl tears
and turn them into happiness
if you gave me a chance

I should have said those things
but it was too late
your train had already left

Originally published 4/27/2010 on vox poetica:
http://poemblog.voxpoetica.com/2010/04/27/things-i-should-have-said.aspx

The Travel Guide

Jennifer Bierhulzen

As he stood near a bench in the terminal waiting for his entire group to assemble, the guide mused, "Why don't these things ever start on time?" After looking at his watch, he glanced at his list for the umpteenth time and noticed that everyone was accounted for except one. He mumbled under his breath, "There's always that one percent who can't seem to get here when they're supposed to."

A little girl with clear blue eyes walked up to him and said happily, "This is so exciting! Do you think that we'll be leaving soon?"

The handsome guide looked down and noticed how pretty the girl was with her golden hair and bright smile. She was probably around the age of ten or eleven and it was obvious that she was anxious to get going. She was brave, considering she was traveling without her parents or siblings to accompany her.

He squatted down in front of her and said, "Well, little one, we are still waiting on someone to get here, but as soon as he arrives, we'll be leaving right away."

She smiled at him, then turned away and went to play with another member of his group.

He wandered a few steps to see how the other travel guides were doing with their groups. It was a large terminal with lots of people moving constantly around. He spied his buddy, Gabe, over in one corner with a group of about fifteen individuals, and he noticed that Michael was already leaving with his group. Somehow, Michael always seemed to get all the members of his group together relatively on time.

"Good for him," thought the guide. "At least he'll be getting back at a reasonable time. Maybe I'll call him later and see if we can get together."

Turning and walking back to his group, he ran his finger down his list and tried to match up the faces with the names. As usual the group was made up of a variety of individuals. Many were either sitting patiently or lying down on the benches. He grinned when he saw that Alice C. Littleton, mother of three from a small town in Virginia; Susan Ann Watts, a legal secretary; and Jurgen W. Betke from Hamburg, Germany, were all engaged in an animated conversation. He was glad to see that Bertha Woodard, a widow from California, was watching the two children in the group. One child was the little girl that the guide had talked to earlier, Sally Simpson, and the other was Tyler Fitzgerald, a young boy with bright-red hair and freckles sprinkled across his cheeks and nose.

He stopped studying his travel members when he noticed that one of the young teen members in his group seemed agitated and distracted.

"Hmmm, what's that boy's name?" he thought. He returned to his list of names and ran his finger down the column until he found it.

"Ah, here it is. Jamal J. Washington or J.J. as most of the group called him, fifteen years old." The guide looked back up and saw the young man nervously strumming his fingers on his leg and tapping the ground with his foot. The guide knew that J.J. had once been a member of a gang, so maybe all the chaos of the terminal was agitating him. "Maybe I should see if there is something I can do for him," the guide thought.

Just as he was taking a step in J.J.'s direction, a spry old gentlemen with a huge grin came walking up and announced, "Whew, I'm finally here. I am so sorry that you had to wait on me, but everyone wanted to say goodbye, and they just wouldn't let me go until they did."

The guide smiled back and asked him his name and personal information.

"Elmer T. Campbell," the senior replied excitedly. "I'm eighty-eight years old, and I've been wanting to go on this trip for so long that I can't believe that I'm really here. Glory be, when do we leave?"

The guide put a check next to Mr. Campbell's name, then folded the list and stuck it in his pocket. He motioned to the rest of the group members to come forward and gather around him, as they were finally able to leave the terminal.

Clearing his throat, he shouted, "Now that everyone is here, we can proceed. Please stay together, especially on the platform, since it is important that we don't end up on the wrong train. Although the ride isn't too long, I suggest you sit back, relax, and enjoy the scenery along the way. After we get there, feel free to explore the sights all you want. The gardens are especially lovely this time of year. As you're ready, take the path through the woods on the far side of the gardens and follow it to the gate at the end. It has been my pleasure to assist you, and I am confident that you will enjoy your trip. Now, if you will please follow me."

The travel guide led the thrilled group toward a tunnel opening at the far side of the main terminal that would lead them to their designated platform. As he walked, he looked up and marveled at the wondrous rays of bright light that were streaming through the windows overhead. Not paying attention, he accidentally slammed sideways into a solid column.

"Oh look a feather," cried Sally Simpson as she picked up a large white feather that came floating to the ground in front of her. "Isn't it lovely, Tyler?"

"Come on children," Bertha chided, "we mustn't get lost from our group. Oh there they are," she said as she pointed to the others a short way down the platform.

Just then the thunderous noise of an incoming train permeated the platform air as it roared into the terminal, brakes squealing. The overhead speakers announced the arrival of the new train to the various parties on the platform.

"All aboard on the Pearly Gates Express!"

30th Street Station

D.C. Ackerly

Time has stopped for me

There is only before and after

Light streams in through long fretted windows

People are all around

But I exist in silent darkness, alone, frozen

I understand those looks now

The tired pained expressions

Searching for hope where there is none

Please someone send me a lifeline

Pull me from the murky deep

But no one is there for me now

She never will be again.

Making Change
Cynthia Siira

" Your change is two dollars and twenty-six cents. One, two, twenty-five, twenty-six. Thank you!" Debi flashed a big smile at her customer and in return for the cup of coffee received a semi-grunt with no eye contact. She ignored the response. She was used to the grunting, the semi-rude, the rude, and the downright rude comments from customers. It was a part of the job. But she had decided years ago to make this negative aspect into as much of a positive as she could. She was friendly to all her customers, no matter how grouchy they were, with the objective of trying to change their mornings.

She had read somewhere that a smile given to someone will spread exponentially, one person starting the happy greeting, the recipient passing it on to someone else, and so on and so on. And she had liked that idea. She thought of her smiles spreading through Philadelphia and beyond, from one face to another, a scattering of good feelings like drops of sunshine throughout the entire East Coast—maybe even farther—maybe all the way around the world. When she was in a good mood, that was what she thought about, and it made her happy just thinking about it. The thought of making a positive change in your own life was such an exciting thing. And maybe she would play a little part of making someone else's life just a little bit better.

Debi came to work every weekday from 6 a.m. to 2:30 p.m. despite rain or sunshine or snow or garbage strikes, whether she wanted to or not. Today she was not having a good day and would have preferred not to be there at all. She was having a hard time making her greetings genuine, having a hard time buying her own smile theory. It just did not work today. She had not slept well the night before as she had worried about the future and her finances (which always seemed worse at three in the morning), so had started out the morning feeling grouchy. She had run out of toothpaste, misplaced her car keys, almost got to work late, which she hated, and she seemed to have more rude customers this morning than usual. It just was not a good day, and her sleepless night did not help her cope with customers.

There was a lull in the run for coffee, and she took the time to look at her surroundings. Kofee Kwik, right in the middle of the Philadelphia's 30th Street Station, looked very small in the vastness of the terminal. People scurried about, going from one place to another, flowing around the kiosks like water rushing around islands in a large stream. She watched the people as they hurried by. She looked enviously at the young women striding confidently across the concourse with their computer cases and large business-style purses. They were going somewhere important, doing important things, making important decisions. They wore such nice clothes, boots and shoes, and had fashionable makeup and hair styles.

They could afford all those things. Debi could afford little at this point in her life. She had enrolled in college. Just thinking those words "going to college" gave Debi a thrill, even today when she felt down. Her children were in college themselves, thanks to financial aid. Being divorced years ago, she had no one at home to worry about. She had started to work on her own dream—getting her business degree.

Actually, she was still working out specifically where her dream would take her. It continued as a work in progress, being molded and encouraged as she pursued it. Some days she didn't feel that she was chasing down her dream. Some days she felt that she played hide-and-seek with it; other days she had to round it up and beat it with a stick to get it going. Making a dream happen was hard work. She had read one of Thoreau's statements in her literature class: "If you have built castles in the air, your work need not be lost; that is where they should be. Now put the foundations under them." Debi liked that statement a lot and had written it inside her notebook. She was building her castle's foundation and carrying all that figurative brick and mortar could be tiring and often disillusioning. But on she trudged, her smile theory and Thoreau helping her get through the days of endless cross people and low pay.

She had married just out of her teens and had children right away. Her life had been full and busy with her husband, children, and life in general for many years. When Jacob, her youngest, headed off to the university, she had wondered what she would do next. She had jokingly said to Jacob, "I should go to college too. Everyone else is going." And Jacob had said "Why not?" They had laughed, but Debi thought about it for days. Truly—why not? Why not go to college? And she started building the foundation of her dream—whatever that might be.

Sometimes she thought she might have her own business. She often thought what she would do to make Kofee Kwik a better place to work. She would definitely change the name. She absolutely hated the name. Kofee Kwik. Were the owners so quick they couldn't spell correctly? Or were the customers in such a hurry they couldn't read all the extra letters in the correct spelling? Or were they going for the alliteration? Whatever. It didn't work for her. No, if she were to have a coffee shop with a cute short name she'd choose *Café Vite*. That was also Coffee Quick, but in French and short (for those readers in a hurry) and easy to say. The next name she would change would be her own. Her given name was Deborah, and she liked her name. In middle school she had changed her name to Debi—with an "i", which she had sometimes dotted with a circle or a heart or flower. The name had stuck. One should not have to be saddled with a name chosen in middle school. What a ghastly time of life. Maybe, in the future, in her new job with her new education, she would change to Deborah. A new life with a new name. She liked that idea. But she was still in school and she didn't own a coffee shop. She just worked in one. This one. She would be working here and would be in school another year. Today, that long year seemed to be stretching out endlessly ahead of her. She did not know if she would have the energy or the enthusiasm to keep going.

Her thoughts were interrupted by a young man.

"Excuse me? Ma'am?"

She looked up, ready to take the order. He looked at her name tag and said, "Debi, the lady who just left, she forgot her laptop. I tried to catch her, but she disappeared, so I brought it right back here. She'll probably be back. Would you be able to hold on to it?"

"Of course!" Debi reached across and pulled the bag onto her side of the counter. "How nice of you to do that! Not everyone would have been so honest! Thank you so much. I'll keep it safe back here. Could you tell me what she looked like? So I give it to the right person."

"I can't tell you much. About thirty. Shoulder-length, light-brown hair. Kind of pretty. Sorry, that's about all I can do. Oh, and she was wearing a black coat."

That pretty much described twenty-five percent of the women who breezed through the terminal every day. Not much help, but he had at least tried.

"I'm sure that will be fine. I hope she comes while I'm on duty. If not, I'll let the next shift supervisor know." She handed him a free coffee—with the warm smile she gave to everyone. "Goodness may be its own reward, but it doesn't hurt to have a little extra, don't you think?"

She'd have to pay for the coffee out of her pocket, but he'd done a good deed and should be thanked. She'd be rewarded in turn by giving this young woman her laptop back, not a monetary reward, but thanks and a smile. She gave a lot of smiles and got so few in return. Not real ones anyway. She looked forward to the appreciation and thanks that would be coming. Debi looked at the crowd and wondered how long it would take for Laptop Lady to realize that she'd lost her bag. She must've had a lot of things with her to leave that behind. Some people live and die by their laptops. Thinking of the young man who'd returned the computer, and the happy scene when the computer would be given back, made the next hour of Debi's day go by more quickly and pleasantly.

Soon another hour passed. Debi was concerned that her shift would be up before Laptop Lady returned, and she wanted to be the one who returned the computer. She had hidden it behind a case of cups so no one could get to it without her knowing. Perhaps it was silly and selfish, but she wanted to be the one to receive the thanks. She had been the one to hold on to the laptop, and who had given the young man his coffee. It should be she who would reap the reward. Three hours went by, and Debi continued to smile and serve coffee, but she quickly scanned the lobby every couple of minutes, looking for a young woman with light-brown hair and a black coat.

As the fourth hour approached, Debi knew that Laptop Lady was coming her way. There was determination in her step and a frown on her face. She pushed her way to the front of the line and asked brusquely, "Did anyone turn in a laptop here this morning? I left it here."

Finally, Debi would get the thanks she had been waiting for all morning.

With anticipation, Debi pulled the laptop case from behind the box of cups and lifted it over the counter. "Here you go. I was hoping you'd get here before I got off this afternoon."

"Right. Has it been dropped?" Laptop Lady snapped as she pulled the case toward her.

"Not that I know of. Not since I've had it back here." Debi responded with her usual cheerful response.

"Okay." And Laptop Lady strode off the way she came.

No thank you. No return smile. No nothing. Just rudeness.

Debi just stood there looking after her, speechless. Her disappointment melded with her exhaustion, and together they overwhelmed her. Then, her thoughts finally coalesced. Well. I'm done. No more smiles. No more stupid smile theory. No smiles are going around the world. They don't even make it out of Philly. No, they don't even make it past Kofee Kwik. I'm done. Her shift ended. She signed out and went to class and went home and went to bed. And she didn't smile all evening. It was too much work.

She dreaded going to work the next morning. She didn't know how she was going to handle all those irritable people before they had their coffee. She didn't have her usual smile defense to help her get through her day. It would be eight long hours of one face after another, one cup of coffee after another. She hadn't realized how much her theory had helped her until it was gone. The remaining year now seemed impossible to get through, just too tiring, too many grouchy people, no thanks for doing well. But she didn't have another job, so she had to go to work. And she went, like she always did. With a heavy heart, she started what she knew would be a long day. The hours passed. People bustled from one train to another, in and out of the cavernous terminal. Debi, in the center of it all, provided quick and courteous service, no more and no less, giving coffee and change with automated efficiency. She did her job. There was no joy, nothing to look forward to except the end of her shift. And then tomorrow it would all start all over again.

"Ma'am? Did the lady ever come back for her laptop?"

Debi looked up from the register, and her eyes focused on the young man who had found the laptop.

"Yes, she did," she replied politely.

"I'm glad. I was wondering. But I also wanted to come by to thank you. You gave me that cup of coffee yesterday, and it just made my day. I thought about it several times yesterday, and it made me smile." He looked rather sheepish. He shrugged, "Anyway, I just wanted to tell you thank you. Not very many people are that nice." The young man smiled, a genuine smile that radiated from his eyes.

Debi felt the sincerity of his thanks. The young man's response reminded her of all the people who had smiled back at her, who had been pleasant, even though in a hurry. Who knows, people may have needed her friendly greeting just as she had needed the young man's thanks. As she continued to work her shift, she thought about her job, people, and just life in general. By the end of the day she was greeting her customers with a friendliness they felt. Her smile theory was back.

The next morning at work, Deborah put on her new name tag. I may as well make small changes as I go. No sense leaving them all for after graduation. Then, she smiled at the next customer as she counted out the change.

Old Woman at the Train Depot
Ruby E. Pruitt

No one seemed to notice the old woman sitting on the bench at the depot. She told some folks as they walked by, "I'm waiting for a special train!" Whether they noticed her or not did not really seem to bother her. After all, she was told to come here and wait for that special train.

She seemed a kindly old lady. For all I knew, she could have been someone's grandmother. Dressed in her finest suit, her only luggage was a carpetbag near her side. She told a stranger who sat near, "Today I go on a wonderful train ride!"

I listened as she rambled about "previous days gone by."

"My momma and daddy used to bring me here years ago when I was just a child. Oh the fun we used to have as we sat on this very spot! The depot isn't as it was then. Folks would rush to get their tickets so they could get a good seat on the train. Transportation was a lot different back then for there were no buses, cars, or airplanes.

"Those old engines would take us to town or other places. Sometimes the coal-powered engines would bring us back. Our clothes would sometimes get covered in soot as we rode down the track listening to the train go clickety-clack!"

The old lady pointed to a spot and said, "Sometimes I'd get licorice candy from a vendor over there. If we knew the circus was coming to town, we'd rush to see the circus train go by. Oh my, that seems like only yesterday, but it was really so long ago. How time just seems to fly!"

Her voice seemed to fade as she remembered her past. I wondered how old she really was as the sunlight shone through the window onto her neatly styled silver hair. "This place holds such fond memories for me," she said as she wiped away a tear. I was in no hurry so I sat silently and listened as she rambled.

She talked of meeting the love of her life in this very place. She also spoke of him catching a train to go off to war. Then another tear ran down her sweet face. She brightened, though, as she spoke of the day her soldier came back home with a ring and a proposal for her. "He couldn't wait until later, no sir." He had to ask her hand in marriage as soon as he could. So glad to have him safely home, she said, "yes," right where she stood.

This depot seemed to be very much a part of this woman's life, I thought, as I continued to listen. She reminisced about visits when she brought her children just to watch the trains go by. Sometimes, they would sit and watch the people as they bustled about the busy station. Occasionally, someone important would come through, and it gave the children a great thrill, especially if it was a president or some other famous person.

She seemed to long for those days gone by, when folks were much more caring and when manners were used. Folks really meant it when they asked how someone was faring.

"Oh how the styles have changed over the years!" she exclaimed.

"What was your favorite one?" I asked.

"Whatever was decent. I never went for the fancy frills. The glitz and glamour never really impressed me. Simple yet elegant is how I choose to be! I'm not out to impress anyone. I like who I am," she said with a smile.

"Do you see that spot over there? It used to not have all that fancy tile. 'Twas all hardwood floor at one time. Now just look how that stuff shines, especially when the sunlight hits on it. They really have fixed up this old place since my last visit here," she said. "Such big old windows to let more light in I guess."

She paused, hung her head, and said, "You know, folks come and go in and out of our lives. The older you get, certain things just don't seem as important as they used to be. Like getting all the dirt off the floor or the dust tats off the ceiling. The important thing is to live a right life—enduring and forgiving others during toils and strife. But most of all, knowing God and living a life that pleases Him."

The woman then fell silent as she paused a long time. She slumped back against the wall. Her eyes had another look now, for death had come to call. She had taken one final ride. The Lord took her hand, for her special train had finally come. She rode her last train and left for her final home.

A Modern Train Station

D.J. Christiano

The train was running late. I was not surprised. The Crescent always ran late; it was two hours this time. At least I didn't have to rush to get to the Manassas Train Station. It was Sunday, and I thought traffic on Route 66 would not be an issue. In reality, I knew anything can happen when you travel east on Route 66, even on a Sunday. We left the house early as planned.

I checked with Amtrak on the way to Manassas. The train seemed to be gaining time, now only about an hour late. Perhaps arrival at our destination, New York's Penn Station, would be close to the posted time. I wanted to spend as much time in the Big Apple as I could. There were always so many things to do, and I just didn't want to waste a New York minute.

As we boarded the train, I asked the conductor about arrival time. He assured me that we would arrive as scheduled. I didn't have much confidence in that statement until I sat down. The scenery flew by. As we approached Penn Station, the conductor winked as he walked by; we had arrived on time. He definitely knew something I didn't.

Hours vanished as we toured the battleship Intrepid, took in a ball game at Yankee Stadium, spent time rubbing elbows with the Beatles, Donald Trump, and Bon Jovi at Madam Tussaud's Wax Museum, and, of course, shopped. After two fun-filled and exhausting days, it was time to check out of the hotel and head home.

While my husband was packing, I turned on CNN to get a quick update on current news. I hate to admit it, but I am a CNN junkie. I manage to find a CNN station no matter where I am. Even on cruises, I tune into CNN International a few times a day. After I watched the scroll for a few seconds, I saw the alert. "Cameras at Penn Station, Times Square, and Grand Central Station are now broadcasting in real time." I knew that when "real time" was broadcasting anywhere there was a security threat. (I learned that on a CNN news special).

    I told my husband to hurry. I was ready to get out of New York and back to the safety of Culpeper. My husband was not moving fast enough for my liking. He told me he would rather wait at the hotel than at Penn Station. The train was not scheduled to leave for another hour. I informed him that the 38th floor was way too high for the NYC firemen to rescue us. We left in the next five minutes. I could instill fear and terror in anyone. I also wanted to walk by the CNN office building to see if anyone interesting was coming out or going into the studio. And I was interested to see if any last-minute alerts were posted. No Anderson Cooper or Wolf Blitzer was in sight. No further news announcements ran on the outside scroll.

    We arrived at Penn Station without any excitement. I settled in a chair in the waiting area. My husband went to get some snacks for the trip back. I saw all trains to DC were on time. The waiting room was not crowded or noisy. It was quite calm compared with the last few days of pushing crowds, honking horns, sirens, and police whistles. My thinking about our activities in New York was interrupted by a routine announcement that droned over the intercom. An alert soon followed, "Please alert security if you see any unattended packages or luggage." The voice sounded different from the general announcements. My husband said that was my CNN imagination at work.

    While he read the newspaper, I scanned the waiting area and noticed one man making a business call, another working on his laptop, an older couple taking a cat nap, and a young lady with too much luggage. Where was she going with all that stuff? She had five suitcases, one green string-tied bag, and a red igloo cooler with a rather large black chain around it. I interrupted my husband's reading about the Yankees.

"What do you think is in that cooler? She has such a big chain around it with an oversized lock," I said.

He replied, "Probably a special beer. Here, have a cookie and mind your own business."

The lady stood and gathered her things together. I wondered how she would get all her luggage on the train. Another woman hurried to help. It looked as if they were traveling together. They managed to get everything rolling, but left the cooler and green sack. I ran after them to remind them of their forgetfulness.

"The cooler is not ours, neither is the green bag. They were both there when we sat down," was the reply.

My brain went on Red Alert! I looked around for security. No security. I hurried back to my husband to alert him. I asked him to go and find security. He said he would as soon as he was finished with the paper. By that time, we could be dead. I went to locate a security agent. Not only did I find a security guard, but four fine young men from the National Guard, fully armed in flak jackets and with dogs.

"Okay, do not panic. No one else is screaming terrorist attack. Keep your cool. Speak slowly and carefully," I said to myself.

I told the guardsmen about the red igloo. They took me seriously and looked concerned. I was told to stay put as they hurried toward the suspicious package. I saw my husband put down his paper, grab the two suitcases and walk, rather quickly, to where I was standing. He wanted to wait closer to the exit. I agreed.

With their handlers, the dogs ran from the station. They were now going down to the train platforms. Everyone cleared a path for them. We soon saw more officers rushing to the waiting area with a large metal container.

A Train of Thought

I held my breath and looked at my husband. His face looked very concerned as he told me that now all the trains to DC were running late. Our train had "standing by" next to it on the departure listings.

Everyone remained calm and stared at the departure board. No one said a word. Is this how people handle fear? Stoic, resolved to impending fate, brave. I felt sick to my stomach, immobilized with fear, and not able to think very clearly.

The bomb squad officer sped out of the waiting area with the metal cart. The situation was resolved. Lines were forming at the food stands as the announcement of train arrivals and departures resumed. I started to breathe normally. My feet responded to putting one foot in front of the other as we walked to the train platforms. The train went a lot slower back to Manassas, taking two hours longer than the train we took to get to New York. I didn't care. The ride gave me some time to reflect.

Although I'll never know if either package was harmful, I am happy that I acted on my gut feeling that day. How many times have things been "taken care of"? We'll just never know, not even CNN.

Faces in Stone

Ghostly stone cherubs peering out the window of a Charleston art gallery left their imprint on these authors—best read during daylight hours.

Photograph: © Jack Daily

Wanderings of Self
Bobbie Troy

i wander through the graveyard
seeking my true self

perhaps i am a ghost
embodied in a stone statue

perhaps i am a soul
that rises with the morning mist

perhaps i am an image
trying to define itself

perhaps i shall see my self
reflected in the eyes of the dead

but perhaps my wanderings will take me
outside this yard of graves
to the one and only place
to discover my true self

While Eavesdropping on Two Cherubs
Ruby E. Pruitt

I saw two cherubs talking the other day. I leaned in close for I was curious about what cherubs would have to say.

"You took the other one, didn't you?" the one cherub said.

The other cherub blushed from head to toe in a lovely shade of red. Ah ha! Guilty as charged I thought—or could I have been misled, by the blush of that second cherub who turned to the other one and said, "It isn't exactly as you think. Although I thought my action had been hid, I'd rather not explain as to why I did what I did."

The first cherub then asked, "Well, why are you blushing then?

Your blush makes me think you are guilty, not innocent!"

To which the second replied, "Oh but I really didn't take it you know!"

The second cherub blushed again in that shade of red from head to toe.

"It's just that if the truth were revealed,

The guilty one would know!" the second one squealed.

As they paused, I took a bite of my snack,

A cookie I had found placed in my backpack.

After a moment the first cherub said,

"Then why do I see chocolate on your forehead?"

"Oh dear," the second replied.

"Okay, I'm caught, I kinda sort of lied.

But I took the cookie only to give someone a snack.

So I took it off the plate and put it in their backpack.

I knew they would get hungry you see,

So I thought I would show them some kindness, you know, do a good deed.

I really didn't see any harm,

As for the chocolate on my forehead, when I took it, the cookie was still warm."

I was really enjoying my snack,

That cookie I had found placed in my backpack.

As I realized what that cherub had said,

It was my turn to blush in that lovely shade of red.

For it finally dawned that the guilty one was me,

As I finished off my chocolate chip cookie! The moral of this story is,

When on a conversation you listen in,

Think twice before a word is heard,

Listening in on others uninvited can be a lesson learned.

Two Cherubs

Judith Dreyer

I am so mad at him! Furious is a better word. Oh we had a good life, the best, but I'm not talking about that. What I'm saying is that he went first. He left me behind, and I can't stand it. I want to handle this more gracefully, but there is nothing graceful when the love of your life is taken. I'm tired of crying, yet the tears come anyway. There are no soft touching words to ease this place I'm in so please ... don't ... try.

Eddie and I were high school sweethearts. I have no idea what stars we were born under, but we were meant for each other. We pretty much knew that at sixteen. We discovered, among other things, that we loved the forest and gardens and plants. Eddie got a job at Mr. Beckwith's Nursery that year and did much of the grunt work. I worked at Spaulding's Florist, learning floral design. He dug the soil while each bead of sweat brought him closer to a dream. I hauled buckets of rotten stems that became like a perfume that scented my dream. We started saving and made plans for a time when we would break away to begin on our own.

Now understand, my parents wanted me to go on to college. Eddie's parents wanted him to take over the family business selling appliances. But we wanted our own gardens and our own business. We would sit for hours after work and imagine antique hedge roses over every fence we would have, and we wanted plenty. We dreamed we would plant fruit trees in honor of each child's birth, and we wanted three. College could be down the road, but we had to have our garden bloom first.

Resistance, they say, makes the heart grow stronger. The opposition we felt from family only toughened our resolve and break away we did. Oh, we weren't foolish enough not to finish high school.

We did. But when our eighteenth birthdays rolled around, we acted on our plan.

Eddie turned eighteen first in mid-spring. He was a late bloomer and probably put on six inches our last year in high school. His six-foot frame towered over my petite five-foot-two inches. I turned eighteen that July. We had been saving for two years now. Eddie talked with Mr. Beckwith about our plans. Christmas in July, the 25th, marked the day of our wedding. Mr. Beckwith convinced Miss Spaulding to help us at the courthouse. We got married and then broke the news to our folks. What could they do? Not much, as they say. We had the paper and the resolve to stand firm like the pin oaks that grew around our first home.

Mr. Beckwith owned an empty cottage down the road from his home by a stream near the forest's edge. He offered it to Eddie and me. Ten feet by twenty with a boat-sized sink, it was our first home. We headed there after our wedding vows were spoken and ate the sweet lunch Miss Spaulding had prepared.

Happy and giggling, maybe even a bit shy, we drove down to the cabin and eagerly got out of the car. Holding hands, we walked slowly to the front door, hardly believing this day had arrived. Were we surprised when we spied two statues, one on each side of our front door, the only door I might add. A boy placed on the right and a girl on the left. I looked at Eddie and caught him grinning from ear to ear. Somehow we knew Mr. Beckwith had something to do with putting these two cherubs by our front door as a wedding surprise.

We were avid readers and loved to tell stories. The ancient myths kept us entranced during those two years prior to our wedding when we worked and planned. We would often spin a yarn or two about our lives as we waited for this our wedding day to arrive. Eddie was the better storyteller, and I could listen to him for hours. He would coax me to add my two-cents worth, but it was his deep, resonant voice I remember filling the room with adventure. Before Eddie carried me over the threshold, he insisted we name these playful figures. We decided they would be our personal guardians. Each item they held was a gift from the gods, a talisman that would bless our lives. Eddie picked Osiris, and me, well I chose, Isis, for the girl figurine. Noble names for these figures made of cement, but we wouldn't let their youth dampen our high aspirations. Giggling, my Eddie carried me through our front door decorated with roadside wildflowers I picked the day before.

I think you can see the picture? My Eddie is my Osiris. The cancer got him, and while his body broke, he continued to tell me stories. After all our years of struggle and success, the ups and downs that create a life, I still hear his voice. While we saw our dreams of home and hearth expand and actually created the gardens of our imaginations, the statues were a part of this life we wove and became old friends. Once they marked the entrance of our vegetable garden, adding grace to chicken-wire fencing.

Then, we began a tradition. We would secretly place the statues by the front entrance as each of our kids got married. We had three. With each wedding, these cherubs found new homes, conferring the blessings Eddie and I held in our hearts for our sons' and their wives' new beginnings.

Now, having made their way back to me, the statues sit by the shed. The kids gave them to me when Eddie passed. Though they look used and worn to you, to me they hold the stories and the charms that graced our life. I come back here to sit and remember. My hands ache, but I still love to trim the rose hedge. I find Eddie here in the sweet scent of the blossoms and the anger dissolves. I look for him here, and my heart still aches. I so wanted to piece him back together his last months. But I couldn't and I can't, at least not yet. I know that when it's my turn to go, these sweet guardians will carry me home to my Eddie. We'll be whole and complete again.

Treasured Faces
D.J. Christiano

I walked through rooms brimming with precious possessions and stopped to admire two treasured faces. Their worn expression made me question: "Where had they been? What had they seen?"

A weathered look peered through the veil of age that covered their faces. I imagined years spent in summer's blinding sun and winter's cold hard rains. Had misty showers touched their cheeks or howling winds shook the foundation on which they stood?

In my mind's eye, I could see them majestically stand guard over a garden bursting with nature's beauty, happily being a part of an old southern garden. Had each been a proud sentry for the colorful flowers planted with care by women who later sipped iced mint juleps with gloved hands? Or had each silently ruled over a place in disarray with the absence of beauty where the used leaves of fall hide in the dirty corners of an unkempt work space?

Is each waiting and hoping for the beginning of life to once again emerge from its soul?

Perhaps they, like we, had experienced the beauty and squalor, the serene and strife, the warmth and coldness, the illumination and darkness.

They, like we, had experienced the duality of life.

A Visit With Cherubs

Fran Cecere

I dreamed about you last night. When the alarm rang, I quickly pressed the off button then stayed very still in bed, closed my eyes, and recalled everything about the nighttime vision. I had heard about this technique on television to help remember dreams. It worked. For almost ten minutes, I reveled in the movie playing in my head. You were so tender while we danced together in the soft sand with the waves crashing on the shore. Although we had many romantic dates during the six months we had been dating, this dream was even more loving. It was glorious, but then, I dragged myself out of bed and got ready for work.

It was almost a waste of time for me to be in my store today. It's not that it wasn't busy. There were customers in and out all day. There was still a need for pet supplies, and perhaps because it was the first weekend of spring, people were coming in ready to buy. Whenever I didn't have a customer, I thought about you. Most often, I recalled our first kiss. Your eyes sparkled in the light of the moon. If my eyes sparkled at all, I'm sure it was from wonderment and joy.

I knew you wouldn't be home, but I went to your house at lunchtime anyway. Ringing the doorbell was just a ruse to be on your porch. While on the wooden stairs, I tried to feel your presence even though you have been gone for over a week. I stared at the hanging plants, the shrubbery, and the rose bushes, which were just beginning to get green leaves. Your house looked much like the other houses on the block, but I knew it was very different. There was something magical about this place.

Maybe because the winter snow had finally melted, I saw something on your lawn that I had not seen before. Two cupid-like stone statues seemed to be peeking out from around the bushes.

"Where did you two come from?" I asked, as I walked toward them. Did I expect them to hear me? Although they had chiseled mouths, they were speechless. I knew it made no sense, but when I reached them, I continued to talk. "What have you seen and heard? Who visits this house? What most pleases your master?" I addressed these two stone figures as if they were steadfast guards and held secrets they would tell me if I was just stubborn enough.

I looked at the smaller statue and noticed that she held a little object in her hands. It made me want to find a similar dish made out of gold to give you on our fiftieth anniversary. This thought made me dance. I reached over and touched the male statue. Slowly I twirled around him and flirted.

"Dance with me. Come on little one. Show me what you've got. Give me one little squeeze," I begged him.

I hugged myself as I twirled around. Then, I closed my eyes, lifted my face to the sun and spread my arms high and wide. I felt young, weightless, and dreamy. My dance didn't last very long. I realized neighbors might be watching, but I didn't care. I had waltzed on your lawn with the cutest little man in town, and he would forever keep the dance a secret. I joyfully shouted, "I will do that every spring for the rest of my life." Then I whispered to myself, "Now go back to work."

Twins

Jennifer Bierhuizen

Twins born from death
Both young and sweet
Brother and sister
Now only concrete.

A parent lost both
His anguish was awful.
So he made you together
In hopes to remember.

You stand together,
Siblings suspended in time.
Images recreated,
With details and fine lines.

Your parent is now gone,
But still you remain,
Watching as others go by,
Again and again.

Twins from death,
Why are you here?
Someone moved you it seems,
From graves you stood near.

Poor lost children,
Poor displaced twins,
Stay together, you two,
For as long as you can.

Stuck In Stone

Caryn Moya Block.

For decades did we stand
My brother and I
Upon the site of our eternal rest

Stuck in stone
All alone
Unable to go home

Day turned into night
Night turned into day
Until even our names were forgotten

Then one bright morning the children came playing
Dancing and screeching, running and laughing
Hope was awakened at last

Then with a push and a shove
A wobble and turn, the statues fell
Broken . . . Open

The children screamed and ran
Fearing their mother's tongue
Except one little girl

With a silent smile she watched
As we burst from our tomb
and into our father's embrace

With a wave and a laugh
She skipped down the path
As we turned to the light

Finally free to move on
Our waiting long
Into the beyond

A Look Back

Stories by Windmore writers have been shared for twenty years. This section pays tribute to the writers selected from the first three editions.

1992

Windmore Writers Anthology

George H.W. Bush was President. Gas cost $1.05 per gallon. *Unforgiven* won the academy award for best picture, and Windmore Writers published their first anthology.

Santa Claus Came in a Barrel

Sarah Calvert Hitt

'Twas Christmas 1989, my husband and I were packing a box to go to our eighty-six year-old cousin. No longer did we need to "do" stockings for the children, for now they had children of their own.

This box we would make into a real surprise for a man who lived alone, independently enjoying each day and inspiring his neighbors, his Kiwanis friends, and many associates.

What should go into the box? His material needs were met. We searched to find tokens of our love. Claude brought out a jar of his favorite homemade pear preserves. I decided on a homemade loaf of whole wheat bread and a pound cake made from my mother's recipe—a real prize winner. We chose a sturdy box that had come to us filled with those luscious pears that travel nestled in green cushioning. In the open spaces, we put nuts and tucked in one of the pears.

As we had gotten out the decorations for our tree, we chose several wooden ornaments that would travel safely. One could almost feel the hand of Santa wiggle the bright little red-and-green miniature wagon, the jumping jack, and the sleigh into the niches.

There seemed to be that hidden spirit right there in the room with us. We added a small beribboned wreath with tiny apples and closed the sturdy lid to the box.

How should we send it? The Post Office is good, but we wanted it there in time—as though it slid right down the chimney.

UPS was the answer. We chose the two-day delivery between Virginia and Massachusetts.

Our hearts felt warmer, and the childhood wonder of the unseen filled our thoughts. The real meaning of Christmas filled our quiet household.

We returned to the busy activities of visiting, dining, and exchanging gifts.

Then, the postman left a letter. Our package had arrived on time. No doubt, Santa Claus had made a star performance from the way our cousin described his surprise and enjoyment.

But little did we know how his joy would come back to us.

This package had recalled for him the Christmas when he was six years old—yes six—eighty years before.

My mother and father lived on a high hill that sloped to the Rappahannock River. The river was the means of transportation. Steamboats were essential.

The way he told it, our cousin's father had gone to the wharf in Washington, DC, and arranged for delivery to their home of the barrel my folks had shipped.

The barrel, sans wrapping tape, was taken to their kitchen where the burlap top cover was removed to get to the contents.

These contents included homemade cake, fresh fruits—apples and pears—that had been gathered from the orchard and carefully stored in old chest in an unheated room. Walnuts from the trees on the farm, walnuts that had been cracked with a hammer on an old stone rock—a rock that had been used so long that it had a sunken middle. Wild duck gathered by hunters then plucked and dressed, some packages of ham and other pork tidbits—some homemade candies and a Christmas note topped off the barrel.

We felt the warmth that had transpired by sleigh, by UPS, or in a barrel by boat.

The letter from our cousin brought us new insights to the real meaning of Christmas, especially when he closed the letter with "Love—that's what the world needs. Ralph."

1996

Touching the Heart

President William Clinton won his second term. Gas cost $1.22 per gallon. The Academy Award for best picture went to *Braveheart*. Using adult stem cells, Dr. Ian Wilmut and his team cloned a sheep named Dolly. Windmore's second anthology was published.

evening fall

Cora DeJarnette Chlebnikow

remnants of day's warmth
radiate from the still-green ground
bringing up smells of damp earth and grass

a bluebird
silhouetted against the sky
lends his orange and blue hues,
then flying—leave the black

in his place—Oberon
and his firefly entourage
cast a luminous, green spell
charming me into a sound sleep

while thin, white sheet
fog spreads up the hill
and tucks me in.

Our Old Hayloft
John Henry

Our hay loft and barn were each separate and individual places. Oh yes, they were under the same roof and part of the same building—yet two different worlds. Each had its own distinctive smells and characteristics.

Now that barn, a real workplace, smelled of work harness and the barn tenants. Even though the hogs were outside and slept under a lean-to shed, their smells permeated the whole barn. There were the distinctive smells of chickens, horses, and cows. Or should I say, the smells they left behind.

One look at that barn and hay loft would tell you it was unique in the community.

The foundation and framework were made out of peeled pine poles and logs. They were cut and peeled on the farm, and our horse, Dolly, dragged them to the building site. The walls were planks taken from the old clapboard house where we used to live. The roof was made from wood shingles that Dad and I pried out of oak timber, with a maul and froe.

In 1935 Dad got his Veterans Bonus. He took some of that money and built the family a new home. The twenty-eight by thirty-two foot house had five rooms and was sealed inside and out. (No two-by-fours were exposed in the walls or ceiling.) It was the pride of the community, even if it did cost $335. The shingles were made from a new material called Masonite. We had the first Masonite-shingled roof in the county.

Looking back, what that house did not have, seems more important than what it did have. It didn't have water; we got that from a spring. (It was running water. I did most of the running.) It didn't have a closet in the kitchen, bedrooms nor anywhere else. It didn't have a bathroom. It did have a fireplace and a wood cook stove. It was the best house our family ever had.

The Gymnasium

The hay loft was a favorite spot for us five kids. There were good reasons, too. It was the most fun place on the farm—for kids. This is where our slide and gym were built—out of hay, corn fodder, and other forage.

The aroma of new soybean and grass hay is, to the nostrils, "Nectar From the Gods." Combine that with the smell of dried corn fodder and peanut vines, and you have a smorgasbord of wonderful country smells. Oddly enough, the smells of the barn never mixed with the loft smells. However, the loft smells were found throughout the barn.

We would rearrange the bundles of corn fodder to make a "sliding hill." Then, we covered the fodder with grass hay to make it sliding-slick. We spent many a happy hour sliding, rolling, and tumbling on that hay.

The bundles of corn fodder were just right to build playhouses, barns, and forts. We practically grew up in our hay-loft house.

A Special Corner

There was one corner of the loft that was extra special. That's where the peanut hay was stored—with the nuts still on the vines. Mama could tell, when we came to supper, if we had been in the loft. No appetite and a few straws of hay were always a dead give-a-way. To this day, the taste of raw peanuts is a glorious sensation to me. When supper was cooked, Mama would sometimes put a double layer of peanuts in the bread pan and put them in the oven. The wood fire kept the stove hot, and "there is no use in letting that hot oven go to waste," Mama would say. After supper we ate parched peanuts with the family gathered around the fireplace and watched the hulls burn and glow in the wood fire.

What, I ask you, could ever beat the wonderful aroma of fresh parched peanuts? The answer is almost nothing.

Corn Fodder

I enjoyed cutting corn fodder. It must have been "man's work" to me, and that's what made me like it so much. When the corn leaves were about seventy-five percent dry, it was our custom to cut the stalk about two inches above the top ear. We would hold the top of the stalk at the tassel and chop the stalk off using one of Mama's kitchen knives. This action would be repeated until we had a large hand-full of tops. Then we stripped four or five leaves from the bottom of the corn stalk and used them for a tie to keep the bundle together. The bundle was propped on a corn stalk and left to dry. When the fodder was dry, Dad and I would take a plow line (a cotton rope) and head for the corn field. The bundles of fodder would be piled on the rope in big stacks. The rope was belted around the pile tightly and then the pile was stood on its end. We would back up to the bundle, sit on our heels, and pull the bundle onto our backs. Holding the rope with one hand on each side of our head, we balanced the load on our shoulders and headed for the barn. When we arrived at the hay loft, that's when the fun began, at least for me. Harvesting fodder is a hot, hard, and scratchy operation.

The loft door was about nine feet above the ground. The fodder had to go up and into the loft, and we had no lifts. For me, the individual bundles of fodder became Indian spears. I would put two fingers under the tie on the bundle and throw the spear (fodder) as far and high as I could. It was have-to work, but it was fun, too.

When we finally got a wagon, I could throw the spears of corn fodder much farther back in the loft. It still had to be restacked, but the whole harvest operation was much easier and quicker.

It never once occurred to me, in those days, that what I was really doing was building memories for the rest of my life. Now, when I feel that the world is doing me wrong and I want to "Make the World Go Away," as the song says, I stop and think, "I should be kind to this old world; it's where I'll spend the rest of my life."

untitled

Cora DeJarnette Chlebnikow

far above

the stillness of

the murky morning

porch shadows

i hear

a distant engine . . .

something silver

and tempting

trolls past

lightly rippling

fragile contentment

rumbling

fades into

the far off . . .

promising

heat

and cicadas

another summer without a vacation.

unpublished
Cora DeJarnette Chlebnikow

poems are

teeming

tadpoles

desperately darting

waiting,

wishing,

for the status

of a spine

2010
Images in Ink

President Barack Obama started his second year. Gas was $2.73 a gallon. *The Hurt Locker* was the best picture. The sculpture *L'Homme qui marche I* by Alberto Giacometti sold for $103.7 million. You could buy a copy of *Images in Ink* for only twelve dollars.

Cricket in a Jar
Pennie L. Kinsey

Jeramie scampered into the grassy, open field. The breeze whistled through his shirt. The sky was aflame in the late afternoon sun. Today was the day.

Today was his sister Heather's birthday, and he wanted to give her a special present. She always enjoyed sitting outside and smelling the musty leaves in their backyard. But most of all, he knew, she would sit for hours listening to the early evening sounds of birds and insects. Her face would glow with pleasure as she listened to her outdoor orchestra. She seemed to know birds and insects even better than most people who could actually see them. Heather was blind.

So now, Jeramie stood ready on top of the hill, eager to find Heather a pet she could enjoy indoors as well. He was going to catch her a cricket for a pet!

Mr. Quinley, Jeramie's kind neighbor, had just caught up with him. After Mr. Quinley found his breath, he whispered, "Okay boy, remember what I told you now."

Jeramie nodded quietly and scanned the ground. Mr. Quinley had told him that the best places for finding crickets were under rocks, around dead logs, or in tall grass. He listened carefully for the high-tweet sound of the male cricket. Mr. Quinley had said only the males sing.

The field was alive that late summer afternoon with countless birds singing and with the steady hum of numerous insects. It was so noisy that Jeramie couldn't tell which song belonged to the crickets. He knelt absentmindedly beside a gray stone and gently lifted one corner. There, shining black and sleek, was a plump, male field cricket! What a blessing!

Jeramie motioned for Mr. Quinley to join him. They both bent down closer and looked. The cricket began to sing. Jeramie watched eagerly as he saw the cricket scrape one hind wing over another and make a high-pitched tweet, tweet, tweet. The song was so soothing that Jeramie sat totally captivated by the miracle of such a tiny creature's capability.

Mr. Quinley nudged Jeramie gently with his elbow, "Okay now, use the net."

He suddenly remembered his original purpose and swiftly brought the net down over the cricket. Then, he coaxed the insect into the netting and clasped his hand over the opening. The small creature fell into the closed end of the net, and Jeramie smiled proudly.

On the way home, Mr. Quinley explained to him some of the things he would need to do.

"You'll be the one who'll have to take care of the cricket for your sister."

"I do want to take good care of it. What should I feed it?" asked Jeramie.

"When I was a boy, I made sure my cricket had a bottle cap filled with water for him to drink, and I fed him tiny pieces of lettuce, sometimes a bit of banana."

"That sounds great."

"Now then Jeramie, do you have a home for him?"

"I sure do. I've got a big, gallon pickle jar that I washed out. I even made sure there was no soap left inside. Then, I got a piece of old screen to cover the opening, so the cricket wouldn't get out."

"That's good. You know you probably should get some dirt, a few leaves, and a couple of twigs to put in there to make him feel more at home."

"Okay. I will."

"Oh, one more thing. Be sure you clean up after the little friend. Don't leave any leftover food in the jar to spoil. And you can use a little paint brush with a piece of paper to gather up any droppings."

"Thanks, Mr. Quinley, I'll try to remember all that."

They continued to walk the rest of the way home in silence, listening to the cheerful song of Heather's birthday present.

When Jeramie got home, he rushed inside to show his sister her special gift. He found her instead in her favorite chair in the backyard with her face lifted to the remaining warmth of sunshine.

"Happy birthday to you, happy birthday to you," was all Jeramie could sing before Heather laughed and giggled.

"You remembered! I've been memorizing the days until today," she chuckled.

"I have a special gift for you, Heather. Here you are. I bet you'll never guess!" stammered Jeramie.

"Well, what is this? It's round, a lid on top. Mmm. Can I eat it?"

"No," said Jeramie, in stitches.

"What will happen if I shake it?"

"No, don't do that," he said with concern. He wanted the cricket to live at least through the first day.

"Is it a fish?" inquired Heather finally.

"No. Okay, I'll tell you. It's your very own, live, for real, pet field cricket!"

"All for me. Really! Thanks, this is super! I'll even share him with you! We'll have to think of a name to give him. Mmm. Let's think. Hey, how about 'Bit' for 'a little bit of a thing'?" she piped up.

The children sat outside with Bit for a long time until their mom called them for dinner. Heather was so happy. She set Bit up on the table beside her until their dad said, "No."

"But Bit's my birthday present, Dad," cried Heather.

"Heather!" her dad exclaimed emphatically.

"But, Dad!" pleaded Heather.

There was a long, long, long pause. Finally, he said, "Well, maybe Bit can sit under the table next to your feet, but no tipping over the jar. Okay?"

"Gee, thanks, Dad!"

"You're welcome Heather. And say, why don't you lead our evening dinner prayers."

So, Heather prayed: "Dear God, thank you for this beautiful day, for the warmth of the sunshine, for our family, for Mr. Quinley, for this good food, and most of all, thank you for Bit. Amen."

"That was special, thank you Heather," her dad said.

Both brother and sister enjoyed many delightful times together with Bit. Then, several days later, Heather noticed her pet cricket wasn't making as many sounds.

The weather had turned cooler that day, so she had taken his jar outside to enjoy the fresh air.

She wondered how to find out if the cricket was sick. Then she remembered how helpful Mr. Quinley had been to Jeramie. That evening, Heather and her brother went over to the kind neighbor's house to learn why the cricket wasn't singing.

"Well, hi there children, come on in," the smiling gentleman said softly after he opened the door.

"We came to find out more about crickets," Heather said with excitement.

"All right, come and sit down," Mr. Quinley replied, motioning them to choose two comfortable-looking, cane chairs. Jeramie helped Heather locate her seat.

That evening Mr. Quinley showed them a book from his shelf that gave them a few more clues about crickets and how and why they do things. The book, written by Dorothy Sterling, was called *Creatures of the Night*.

There, on page 114, they learned that one kind of cricket, the snowy tree cricket, has a fast song in warm weather, which slows down in cooler weather. That must be why Heather's pet wasn't singing as much, they thought. It had gotten cooler the past few days.

"Hey, listen to this," Jeramie said with amazement.

"Read it, what does it say?" Heather prompted.

As he read, they found out how to tell what temperature it is outdoors by counting the number of cricket tweets in fifteen seconds and then adding forty. The final number is the temperature in degrees Fahrenheit.

"Gee, this is great Mr. Quinley," Jeramie said, bursting with excitement at the newfound knowledge.

"That's a good book, but I also have some notes on interesting things I discovered about crickets when I was your age," Mr. Quinley said, reaching for a large, faded notebook on another bookshelf.

"There must be a lot of information here. It feels like a pretty fat notebook," Heather observed, as she turned over the cover and pages in her hands.

"May we take these books home to read, Mr. Quinley?" asked Jeramie.

"Yes, you sure can."

When they got home, Heather tried right away to guess the temperature by listening to her cricket. It worked! Now they had found a new way of having fun.

From then on, each evening that late summer, Jeramie read to Heather from one of Mr. Quinley's books while her pet cricket sang along happily.

They found out that crickets have "ears" in their knees and that the males sing more if a female is close by.

They even discovered that in China, people carry crickets around their necks while they walk down the street. And they also train some of their prize crickets to fight. Special championship matches are then held, and many people come to watch.

Jeramie was glad that he had learned a lot from Mr. Quinley and from his books. He was also glad because he really wanted to take good care of his sister's pet. And he found out that a cricket is interesting to watch. He was especially grateful the common field cricket is easily found. Most of all, he enjoyed the many hours of enjoyable song and learning the cricket had brought into his sister Heather's life.

Bibliography
Dalton, S., Borne on the Wind: The Extraordinary World of Insects in Flight, Edited by John Kings, Reader's Digest Press, E.P. Dutton & Co., Inc., New York, 1975
Hogner, D.C., Grasshoppers and Cricket, Thomas Y. Crowell Co., New York, 1960, pp. 41-58.
Simon, S., Pets in a Jar, Viking Press, Inc., NY, NY 1975.
Sterling, D., Creatures of the Night, Doubleday & Co., Inc., Garden City, NY, 1960, pp. 103-108, 118.
Stokes, D. W., Nature Guides: A guide to Observing Insect Lives, Little Brown & Company, Boston-Toronto 1983, pp. 200-208.

A Look Back

Patience

Herbert Frisbee

When I was a little child,
And life was bright and new,
The world was filled with things to see,
And much I hoped to do.

My mind was bright and eager,
And my outlook fresh as paint.
All the adults stymied me,
With cautions and restraint.

I was told that I must wait,
For yet a little while.
Or I was much too little,
Such things weren't for a child.

They told me to have patience.
I mustn't be so bold.
Take time to be a kid,
And do as I was told.

I waited. Now the years have flown,
And lately I will smile.
I think of things I want to do,
Like when I was a child.

Those who held me back are gone.
For them the bell has tolled.
But now it's my voice I hear say,
"You can't. Now you're too old."

Photograph: © Jack Daily

Thoughts

MaryAnn Morrison

Today the sun, blocked behind a wall of thunderous clouds, brings no warmth. Familiar sights and sounds filter through my thoughts, as I drag myself out of bed.

After all, it is a day just like many others. It is not a cold-shower day that brings one quickly back from a dream state. It is a day for a warm soak in the tub, releasing the body's stiffness and melting away fears. My morning rituals begin.

As I drink my juice, I think about people I see every day—strangers passing each other without notice, intent only on their own reflections. I wonder which of them grabs a bagel along with the car keys that hang waiting by the door? How many of them are lucky enough to gather around the breakfast table, nourishing body and soul while giving thanks for the day and each other before entering the fray of a constantly spinning world?

Suddenly, I realize how quickly time has passed as the radio interrupts my reverie. "The clouds will be heavy all day," says my favorite weather expert. I pick up my sunglasses anyway, not sure if I am indulging in wishful thinking or just trying to hide the searing pain of loneliness reflected in my eyes.

Fish and Potatoes
Bette Hileman

When I was in elementary school, my parents went on frequent business trips, leaving my sister and me with babysitters. We lived at the bottom of mile-long Tannery Hill in Blandford, a very small town in western Massachusetts.

In early 1947, when I was nine, my parents hired the nearest neighbors, who lived in a tarpaper shack about a quarter mile up the hill, to stay at our house for two weeks and take care of my sister and me. The family—a husband Jack, his wife Eloise, and one daughter Sylvia—heated their home and cooked with a woodstove and ate mostly what they grew in their garden or Jack shot in the woods or fished from streams. Even though my parents knew Jack's family was extremely poor, they thought he and Eloise were kind and would take good care of us. My mother and father were trusting and believed most townspeople would be adequate babysitters for well-behaved children like my sister and me.

Three years earlier, at age six, I'd had an experience with Jack that I had kept secret. About five one spring evening, I was fishing in Bedlam Brook on the west boundary of our property. I was using a fishing pole my father had made—a stick cut from a tree with a line, hook, and lead weight as sinker attached. I didn't know how to fish because no one had taught me any skills.

I was standing alone at the edge of the brook, patiently holding my line stationary in some of the deeper water. As always, I was hoping a fish would see my bait, a worm I had strung on the hook, and bite on it. But, as usual, I hadn't had a single bite.

Jack—a thin, wiry man, wearing jeans and a flannel shirt and high rubber fishing boots—appeared on the opposite bank with his fishing pole. In just a minute, he caught a six-inch trout, a feat I'd never accomplished. He took it off the hook.

"Would you like to have the fish?" he asked.

"Yes," I answered excitedly.

"Well, you can have it if you promise to tell your parents you caught it."

"Okay, I promise," I said with some misgivings.

He walked across the stream and gave me the fish. I left and ran a quarter mile home with my prize.

I handed it to Mother, saying triumphantly, "I caught it."

"Wonderful," she said. "You can eat it for supper."

After my father cleaned the fish, we dipped it in flour and salt and pepper and fried it in butter. During supper, my parents praised me repeatedly for catching the fish. I was already feeling guilty about the lie I'd told them, but believed I would feel even more ashamed if I broke the promise I'd made Jack.

The fish was delicious and convinced me there were great rewards if I could manage to catch some trout.

§ § §

I had my next encounter with Jack in 1947, when he and Eloise acted as babysitters. Each day when my sister and I came home from school, she was peeling potatoes in the kitchen, and he was away hunting or fishing or cutting wood.

Eloise was fat, seventy-five pounds overweight perhaps, and wore loose, unbecoming housedresses. She and her husband reminded me of an illustration I'd seen of the poem "Jack Sprat could eat no fat. His wife could eat no lean."

After peeling for about forty-five minutes, Eloise put the potatoes in a large pot and covered them with salted water. She then boiled them on the electric stove for about half an hour and pureed them with a masher—a hard job with such a huge amount of potatoes.

That was the only thing we had for supper each night for two weeks. With my parents, I was accustomed to eating meat or poultry, salad, green or yellow vegetables, and potatoes or rice at every main meal. Eloise prepared no meat or salad or vegetables other than potatoes.

I was sure my mother had given her enough money to buy a variety of foods. But feeling reluctant to alienate Eloise, I never inquired why we had only potatoes for supper.

I decided either she had no skills in cooking anything except potatoes and occasional fish or game, or she wanted to earn extra money from childcare by serving free food—potatoes stored in her basement. As Eloise and her daughter Sylvia feasted on mounds of potatoes, I thought I understood why they were so fat. Never feeling satisfied from a boring cuisine of almost pure starch, they tried to make up for the protein deficiency by eating excessive calories. Mother and a 4-H cooking class had taught me that the only way to be healthy was to eat a variety of vegetables, meats, fruits, and grains.

Over the next year, I occasionally visited the family at their home and sometimes played with Sylvia outdoors. Each time I walked into their main room, which served as both living room and kitchen, Eloise had a pot of potatoes boiling on the woodstove.

§ § §

The last time I played with Sylvia, I was ten and found myself in trouble again.

It was winter, and the ground was covered with about two feet of snow. Next to the snow banks that lined the steep road coming down

Tannery Hill was a strip of hard-packed snow not much wider than a flexible-flyer sled.

Sylvia, who was a year older than I, said, "Let's slide down Tannery Hill." My parents had warned me repeatedly not to walk or slide on that mile-long hill. It was especially risky, they said, because it was narrow and steep, and had sharp curves near the bottom where cars couldn't see a sled until they were close to it.

"Wouldn't it be too dangerous?" I asked Sylvia.

"No, we'll be fine. I'll keep us right next to the snow bank. Even if a car comes, it can go by us easy."

The temptation of a long, fast ride was too great. Sylvia and I spent twenty minutes trudging up the hill with the sled. At the top, I sat on the front of the flexible flyer and fat Sylvia sat directly behind me and steered with her feet.

We took off. It was a very fast ride. The snow we moved over was almost pure ice on that cold day, and Sylvia weighed more than 150 pounds. She kept us on the two-inch-deep ice near the snow bank, and our rudders didn't break through to the pavement beneath. She also steered carefully around the curves near the bottom of the hill. Not a single car appeared during the trip.

I felt guilty about the escapade but never told my parents about it. Such a confession would have made them extremely angry and elicited harsh punishment, probably a whipping with the belt in the front closet. Also, they would have curtailed my freedom to wander around Blandford for a while.

Although the sled ride had been thrilling—more scary and exciting than any amusement park ride—it had also frightened me. I knew I could have been killed if a car had come along fast behind us, or if Sylvia had not been able to steer properly and veered into the road. I played with her no more after that. I didn't find her interesting and feared she would entice me into even more dangerous adventures.

§ § §

The next news I had about Sylvia's family appeared in the Springfield newspaper when I was twelve. Jack was convicted of raping a thirteen-year-old Blandford girl in the woods and sent to jail for five years. A rape conviction was almost unheard of at the time. Mother told me the incident happened because the victim was "low-class" and probably led Jack on. Then, I felt even worse about Jack, knowing that something awful could have happened to me while he and Eloise were taking care of my sister and me or while I was fishing in streams in the forest. I believed I had through no effort on my part dodged a bullet.

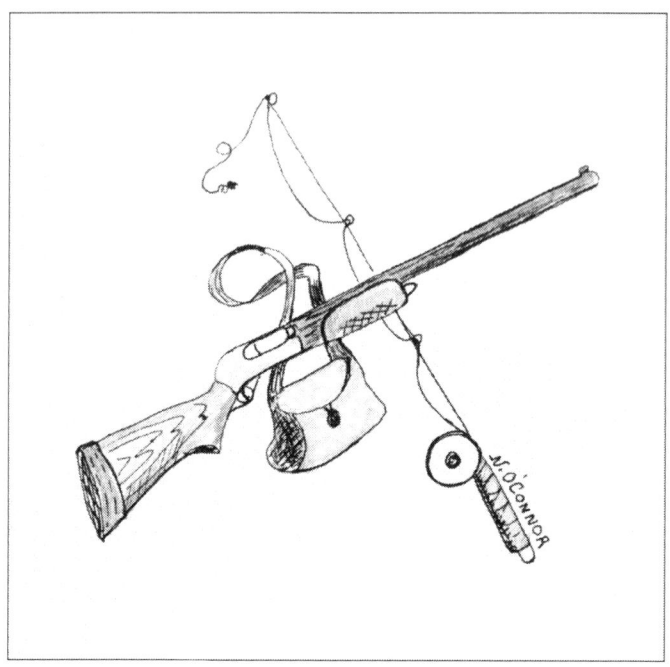

Drawing: © Nancy O'Connor

Bare Huntin'

Herbert Frisbie

My dad is goin' huntin', and it gives me such a scare.
He said when he goes this time, he's goin' huntin' bare.
I don't understand at all, and I sure can't see why,
He'd go without his clothes and things that keep him warm and dry.
He's sure to take his gun and knife, and I know he is tough,
But I can't see how those few things could ever be enough.
I'll talk to Mom, and maybe she can show him there's a reason,
So he'll go huntin' in his clothes and go bare in fishin' season.

Cab Ride
D.C. Ackerly

In his rearview mirror, the cab driver sees a boy sitting in his back seat. The boy is neatly dressed, maybe ten years old. The driver has no children, so he isn't real good at figurin' out kids' ages.

He thinks it's odd to see a kid by himself, but he doesn't want to frighten him off, so he pulls away from the curb. "Where ya headin'?" he asks.

The boy is still for a moment, but then replies with a confident voice, "I'd like to go around the park please."

"Which side, east or west?"

"Start up 8th Avenue. Then turn on 110th Street and come down 5th."

Geez, this kid knows his way around.

The driver looks in his rearview mirror again, wanting a better look at this kid. Maybe he isn't a kid. He could be one of those "little people" or whatever they're calling themselves these days.

The boy's face has a youthful look, and there's something strangely familiar about it, like he's seen him in a movie or something.

But what the driver notices most is the way the boy is staring out the window. He isn't looking up at the many tall buildings as a tourist would. He seems to be captivated by the green leaves on the trees, the yellow cabs, the red traffic lights, and the people walking by in their bright summer clothes.

The driver starts to wonder if this kid's in trouble. Like maybe he's been locked up in an apartment by some wacko for ten years and he's finally escaped. So, trying to get some info out of the kid to see if he should be calling the police or something, he says, "How come you're not in school?"

The boy doesn't answer. He just keeps staring out the window.

When the driver turns onto 5th Avenue, he asks, "You wanna go to the Met or the zoo or somethin'?"

"No," is all the boy says.

After a few more minutes, the driver is getting a bit more concerned that he should be doing something for this kid other than just driving him around. "Look kid," he says. "The meter's turning, and we're runnin' outta park to look at, so how's about I take you to your parents?"

The boy looks away from the window and up at the eyes staring back at him from the rearview mirror. "Just take me back to FAO Schwarz."

"That's good," the driver thinks. Maybe the kid just ditched his rich parents at the store so he could take a little joyride.

Back at the curb, the boy hands the driver a twenty and says, "Thank you." As the driver searches for change, the boy silently slips from the car and seems to melt into the crowd on the busy street. The driver thinks he catches a glimpse of him going through the revolving door into the toy store, but then the boy vanishes like steam from a subway grate.

Scratching his head, the driver starts to remember where he's seen that kid's face before. It was on the cover of a book he'd read in fourth grade.

Looking back at the toy store, he starts to wonder if he has just returned a curious kid to his worried parents. Or maybe he has witnessed a character's release from the confines of his black-and-white pages, who has just experienced color for the very first time.

Unconscious Color

Marlee Laws

Mysterious blue
Tinged red
Betrayal paints away
Purple tries to calm
Hurt is hard to heal
Red is spreading
Blood in a lake of sky
One drop
Obscures the beauty
Never the same
Again, Again
Bitten once
Shy twice
Crimson haze
Heavy as lead
Weighing down my heart
Letting go
Adding white
Adding blue
Lighten the color
Color of my soul
Doubting more
The color
The tinge
That was perfect
Add in black
Darken for safety
Night blanket
Muffles the red
Muffles the sound
Forget
Sleep

The Memory Tree
Fran Cecere

It was getting late, and the campsite was deep in the woods. But the boys wanted a little adventure. Matthew and Daniel, both twelve, were cousins and had been lifelong friends. Their fathers had taken them camping many times, and the boys were active in scouts. On the last evening of the weekend, the boys asked if they could move their tent farther up the hill and camp alone. They wanted to camp just like the big boys they knew they were. Their fathers agreed, but said the boys would have to pitch their tent so they could still see the campfire the men had burning.

Daniel and Matthew grabbed their tent, clothes, and sleeping bags before their fathers could change their minds. Trudging up the hill, they marked the landscape with yellow tape from a roll their fathers had given them and kept looking back to see the campfire. Suddenly, they came upon a small clearing. The grass was lush and green. The boys were surrounded by large trees with thick branches and colorful leaves. This was perfect. They quickly pitched the tent and gathered rocks to make their own fire pit. Each of the boys had been allowed to start a campfire with supervision, so they knew just what to do. Together, they gathered some small, dry branches on the ground under the big trees. It wasn't long before they had a small fire going, but now they needed some bigger logs. They decided to try to break some branches off one of the trees in the clearing. The two boys reached up together and began pulling down one of the limbs.

Just then, they heard a beautiful voice, gently saying, "Don't do that."

The boys stopped and looked at one another. They weren't sure they actually heard the voice or if they were imagining it. Matthew listened, but there was only the sound of tree frogs and leaves rustling in the wind.

"It was nothing," Daniel said, "Come on. Let's get the branch."

Just as they started to pull on the limb again, they heard the voice, "Don't do that." The voice was gentle, yet commanding.

The boys stopped. "Why can't we have the branch? We need it for the fire," Daniel asked.

The voice, which seemed to be coming from the nearby tree, explained, "This is a very special tree. It holds all the memories of every person who ever lived. If you break off that branch, someone's memories will be lost."

Daniel and Matthew stopped tugging on the tree and looked around. "I don't know what you mean," Matthew said quietly.

"Go wrap yourselves in your sleeping bags, and I will tell you," the voice instructed, "and don't worry about the fire. It won't go out."

The boys settled inside the tent, but they could still hear the voice as it told the story of "The Memory Trees."

"Ever since people have been on this earth, they have been gathering memories. Sometimes they can't remember them all so the big trees hold the memories for them. The small twigs you see on the ground are the little things that people forget, like 'don't jump on the bed' or 'don't lose your car keys.' Parents have to tell children all the time to try to remember what their parents have taught them or what they learned in school.

"The large trunks of the trees are the ideas of the great thinkers who have changed the world with their concepts, and these are the things we must never forget. There are also trees that bear beautiful flowers but have long, hurtful thorns. Those thorns are there to remind us about the ideas that are harmful, but the flowers show us that every time we learn a lesson, we can turn the evil around and do something beautiful with the information.

"The colorful leaves on the trees are the most beautiful, sometimes fleeting, memories people have. Every time we see a gorgeous sunset, smell spring flowers, or think about the wonderful things people have done, another leaf is added.

"Sometimes a tree branch dies, gets broken off in a storm, or even gets struck by lightning. These are the memories of older people who have just too much information in their heads or become too old to remember things anymore.

"When a tree or a log is burned, the memories from someone are burned also. Smoke from the fire travels in the air. The smoke eventually reaches a person who suddenly remembers something special about the individual whose memory log is being burned. The memory gives the person a sense of joy and comfort, and then a new memory is formed.

"Sometimes a tree is cut down, and the pulp is used to make paper. That paper is then used to record hundreds of memories so they will be there for generations.

"Try to gather your own memories and pass them on to your family. If you ever need something you have forgotten, go into the woods and spend time among the trees, which are keeping your memories for you. The trees will safeguard your thoughts and give them back whenever you need them."

Reflections

Good writers portray their stories realistically. Truth or Fiction? You decide.

Drawing: © Kathy Webber

Pet Adoption

Diane Burdette

Pressed against a wire door

within a plastic crate

A cold, wet nose

and soulful eyes

Gaze longingly at me.

Each glance and whimper

seem to say,

Please,

rescue me.

The Tiger in the Tile

Pennie Patterson

I was eight when we moved from the tiny apartment to the house on Fern Street. It was a wonderful house! I had my own bedroom. My old top bunk didn't seem the same sitting down on the floor. But there was no Jason in the lower bunk making rude noises, poking his feet into my mattress and generally being a nuisance. It was a good tradeoff.

The best thing about the house was the bathroom. The floor and walls were tiled, and the tile had a swirly, marble-like pattern that I had never seen before. The bathroom had a built-in tub, so easy to get in and out of, quite unlike the ugly thing on feet in our cramped old bathroom. And it had a shower. For days I was so enamored of the shower, I hardly noticed the tile. Gradually, though, I began to find shapes in the beige-on-white swirls. It was kind of like seeing patterns in the clouds. At last, in the back corner, I discovered the face of a tiger.

Its markings were startlingly like those I'd seen in *National Geographic*, right down to the dark shadings on the edges of its ears. It had the wrong colors, of course, but it was a tiger face, and I fell madly in love with it the moment I saw it. I talked to it every time I bathed.

At first, it was just, "Hi, Tiger. How are ya?"—chatter. Then, one night I crawled into the shower completely exhausted and miserable. I'd fallen from my bike, had a terrible argument with my best friend and lost my favorite gloves. I was crying in the shower and poured out the whole story to "my" tiger.

Maybe it was just being able to tell it all without interruption. Maybe it was the comfort of the warm water, or maybe the tiger really was sympathetic as I imagined she was. In any case, I felt much better after my shower. In the days that followed, my "conversations" with the tiger became much more intimate. Tiger heard all my fears, worries, hurts, and joys. Somehow I always felt better after talking to her.

Imagine my horror, then, when four years later my parents announced that as part of their remodeling program, the bathroom would be stripped of everything, including the tile. My arguments about the tile's beauty and easy-cleaning feature went unheeded, except for some nasty jokes by Jason. I cried in the shower again.

That night I had horrible nightmares about a beautiful beige-on-white tiger being chased through the jungle, torn to shreds by shadowy shapes. At one point, I must have screamed out loud because Mom came in to comfort me and ask about my "bad dream."

Of course, I couldn't tell her anything then. I knew big-eared Jason would be awake and blab everything he heard to everyone in school and the neighborhood. He could be such a beast, even today. So I kept it all inside until one afternoon when Jason was at baseball practice and Dad was still at work. Then it all tumbled out. I had to save my tiger. I cried and pleaded and dragged Mom up to the bathroom to see her.

"We've already completed the plans with our consultant," she said finally and showed them to me.

"But you're not changing any of the walls!" I exclaimed. "Why couldn't the tile stay? It would save a lot of money."

In the old apartment days, this would have been a clinching point. But since Dad got this new job, my folks had seemed a lot less stingy about money. I bit my lip, not sure the money issue would be relevant now. Mom sighed.

"I'll talk to your father again," she said, glancing back around the bathroom. "It is rather pretty."

"And unique," I added quickly.

Mom nodded and went back downstairs. I lingered, staring at the tiger face.

"If you know prayers, Tiger," I whispered, "say them now. I'll say some, too."

And we won. The tile with my precious tiger was allowed to stay. The night I heard this news, I had another dream.

A big tiger was caught in a net. A little girl came along. She cut a hole in the net with her sewing scissors. The tiger ran away, and the girl walked on along the path. Some hunters came up behind her. They asked if she'd seen a tiger. She just shook her head. They were very angry. They asked a lot of questions with loud voices. The girl said nothing, only kept shaking her head. At last, the hunters went away. Then the tiger came out of the bushes, walked up to the girl and licked her face. The last picture in the dream was of a beige-on-white tiger face saying, "thank you." I relived that dream often, even in waking hours. It always made me feel better when I was sad.

By the middle of my high school years, my talks with my tiger began to be shorter and less frequent. It was a very busy time that eased my departure for college by distracting me. Before I left the house, I barely found time to say goodbye to the tiger and thank her for all the years of companionship.

In my sophomore year when I came home for winter break, we were snowed in by a huge blizzard. On my second night home, with the wind and snow howling about the house, I had the oddest dream. In it, I was simply sitting in my room, looking from one to another of my favorite possessions and listening to the voice of my tiger asking me why they were always left behind when I was away. I had no answer. Certainly, I had room in my dorm for most of these things. The next day, I began sorting through my stuff. I got an old spare suitcase and packed a lot of little treasures to take back to college with me. At least it helped pass the time while we were snowed in.

Christmas came and went. It was an ordinary holiday—busy filled with food, visiting, and presents. I added a few of these to my treasure suitcase, like the lovely sweater with tigers on it that Aunt Lottie gave me. Had mom told her about the tiger in the tile or was it just coincidence? In our joy at finally being free of the snow and get about, I forgot to ask.

All too soon, the end of my vacation raced toward me. I made sure my favorite clothes got washed and packed, said goodbye to my friends and relatives I probably wouldn't see again until Easter. The tiger's voice in my dreams kept reminding me not to leave behind anything I valued. By my last night at home, I was worried and confused. I had trouble falling asleep, and when I did, the tiger did not remind me of anything. She screamed at me to wake up and get out! I woke about four a.m. in a panic. I smelled smoke! When I opened my bedroom door, I saw light flickering downstairs. The smoke was awful. I pounded on Jason's door, which was nearest, then on my parents' door. At first, they were sleepy and mad. Dad realized the danger at last. He ordered the rest of us to escape while he tried to call 911, but the line was dead.

I raced to my room, put my suitcases out the window onto the porch roof, and scrambled out after them, Jason shoving from behind. I dropped the more-fragile suitcase onto the Forsythia bush to cushion its fall, tossed my clothing down, and slid down the porch corner post a bit too fast after Jason, almost squashing the cat in his arms. Mom and Dad crashed down behind me. The four of us ran as a unit to the Dyers' next door. By now, flames were shooting out the kitchen windows. We had made it out in time, thanks to the tiger's warning. The batteries in the smoke alarms must have been dead because no one remembers hearing the sound.

Fire engines screamed up to the house. At last, they got the fire out. There was a lot of damage, especially to the kitchen and to

Jason's room above it, but the house was salvageable. When the firemen let us go back in, I trudged carefully up the stairs to check out the bathroom. The heat of the fire had loosened the tiger tile. It was singed but intact. Gently, I pried it the rest of the way off the wall, wiped it with tissues, and tucked it in my pocket. The cause of the fire was determined to be a faulty wire in the stove. How had the tiger known?

A day late, I flew back to Atlanta for the winter term at Emory University, all my prized possessions in tow. The most precious possession was the tiger-face tile. That night, I had my last new tiger dream: A huge, magnificent beige-on-white tiger emerged from a forest. She bounded up so that she filled almost my entire vision. As I stared at her, the beige stripes gradually darkened to black. Her eyes darkened, too. When the change was complete, she threw back her head and let out an ear-shattering roar. The familiar tiger voice then cried out, "I'm free! I'm free!" and the beautiful white tiger jumped high in the air before racing back into the forest. I called goodbyes and thanks after her until she disappeared.

My tiger tile has darkened with age. It is almost the color of a regular orange tiger now. Everyone remarks on how lovely and unique it is. They often refer to the tiger as "it" or "him." I don't bother to correct them. I know who she is, and I treasure her above everything else I own. Though I often go to bed thinking of her and hoping to see her again, the only tiger dreams I have are "reruns." Perhaps it is because I now have a wonderful husband who listens sympathetically to all my fears, worries, hurts, and joys. Perhaps it is because one singular angel has finished her work.

The Savior in Cat Alley

Bobbie Troy

Walking home at night down Cat Alley wasn't the smartest thing I ever did, but I liked the sense of danger after sitting at my desk all day. After a while, it became part of my routine. Besides, the mangy critters had come to rely on the treats I brought and scattered on the ground like the loaves and fishes that fed a multitude. Who else would bother with alley cats?

Muttonchops was always the first to come out of hiding. Somehow I suspected that he was the oldest and at one time the meanest, but the fight seemed to have left him along with most of his facial hair. Dainty Dora was always the last to show herself. Black as the night, with only her yellow-green fluorescent eyes showing, she would saunter toward the nuggets of food and slide them gently toward her.

There must have been about a dozen or so cats in the alley at any one time. They would come and go, but Muttonchops and Dainty Dora stayed for some reason.

They weren't much to look at, and nobody cared about them—the dregs of cat humanity. But they were my friends, and they started to trust me. I wonder, who was the savior here?

Drawing: © Martha Harris

What Goes Up

Fran Cecere

The calm of a peaceful Sunday was suddenly shattered by a dreadful crash. I'm not sure everyone would have described it that way, but Mark would have.

Mark Paikin, the kind, generous pharmaceutical representative had been calling on our hospital's oncology practice for many years. We had established a good working relationship that was occasionally enhanced by a glass of wine or conversation over dinner. One day Mark invited my husband Roy and me to join him at the Jamesville Hot Air Balloon Festival. We went on a Saturday and wandered among the many attendees, eating delicious food from the vendors and watching the hot air balloons being prepared for flight. It was a beautiful, sunny weekend, and Mark suddenly got the urge to go up in one of the balloons. However, as hard as he tried, he couldn't find any available flights that afternoon. Finally, he got one gentleman to agree to take us up on Sunday at 8 a.m. if the weather permitted.

Fortunately, the morning was clear with mild winds and blue skies. It was a perfect day to ride in a balloon. Roy and I met Mark at 7 a.m. and found our designated hot air balloonist. The three of us were to be in the basket with the pilot and another couple. We introduced ourselves to the other couple, but after that, we really didn't have much time for conversation. The pilot gave a lengthy safety spiel, and we had to sign a waiver. I realized that if we died on the flight, no one would legally make a dime from the accident. We didn't care. We were too excited. Also, we were out in the middle of a field, and cell phones at that time were bulky, black things that were used in the car. People did not carry them in their purses or pockets. We weren't able to call our lawyers or our families to let them know what the waiver said, so we just signed it and climbed in the basket.

Liftoff was exhilarating. The noise of the burners that made the hot air discouraged any of us from trying to talk. We hung on as the balloon gracefully lifted above the trees in Jamesville, New York. At first, we were not very high. We floated over homes and looked down at people who were drinking coffee in their backyards. They had witnessed the Balloon Festival so many times that it was a part of their Sunday routine on that particular weekend. It was quiet and peaceful. When we saw people watching us, we were able to speak to them and even carry on a short conversation. The views of the Jamesville area were beautiful. There were many other colorful and elaborate balloons in the air that day, and the sight of them with the sky-blue background was breathtaking. We all commented on how quiet it was up there. Mark and Roy occasionally pointed out landmarks to me.

Every once in a while, the pilot called his crew on his walkie-talkie. I realized they were tracking us. They knew the general direction we would travel because of the winds, but they had to take all kinds of different roads just to keep up with us. I felt sorry for them because of the work they had to do while we glided along effortlessly. The pilot occasionally fired up the burner to add more hot air, which made us fly higher.

I lost all track of time, but suddenly the pilot told us the crew had located an open field that was appropriate for landing. He explained that he would gradually let air out of the balloon and it would slowly drop to the ground. The descent toward the grassy field below seemed gentle, almost imperceptible. But as we got closer, we could actually see how quickly we were falling.

Suddenly the basket slammed onto the field. The almost-deflated balloon fell toward the ground where it was caught by the wind. This caused the basket to tip over on its side, and everyone fell. All of us were still in the basket, but unfortunately we landed *on top of Mark*. While most of Mark's body was still in the basket, his face was in the dirt and we were being dragged across the ground. No one screamed or moaned or cried. It all happened too fast. I think I heard a grunt from Mark, but I wouldn't swear to it on a witness stand.

Eventually the basket came to a halt, probably because it had dug deep enough into the dirt. The members of the ground crew ran over and helped us get out. We proceeded to step on the body below us as we climbed, crawled, and clawed our way out. The last person to be pulled out was Mark. His face was grass-stained, but he could still talk. Mark told all of us that he felt he had suddenly become intimately acquainted with the other couple, especially the man, since he was the first person to fall on Mark when the basket toppled over. After that, four more people crushed him. I guess by that time Mark and the other man were no longer perfect strangers.

We were all able to laugh about our experience because no one really got hurt. The pilot gave each of us a glass of champagne to celebrate our first flight. Mark made a big show of spitting out some grass before he took a drink.

As the ground crew got the balloon and basket ready to be transported by truck back to the base, we looked at the torn-up grass in the field where we had landed. Mark made sure to point out that one of the deep furrows dug into the ground was made by his nose when it crashed into the dirt. He showed us his profile so we could admire his proboscis. It didn't look any bigger than it did before the landing. I don't even remember the van that took us back to our cars. Everyone was talking at the same time about how wonderful the experience was.

The best part of this story is it's not exaggerated. It's all true. It is an urban legend in Jamesville. The residents still laugh about this one.

Spinning

Jack Daily

I'm a spinner, not to be confused with a whirling dervish in mystical pursuit. Spinning is my release from the daily grind or sometimes my inspiration to begin the day. I ride spin bikes five times a week in groups as small as four and as large as twelve.

Where do we go on these rides?

Nowhere.

Spin bikes are stationary, which on first thought may seem unglamorous. Dedicated rooms in fitness centers around the country are filled with these bikes. Certified instructors with personalized, up-tempo playlists encourage, cajole, and challenge you to make it the ride of your life.

For one hour, including warm-up and cool-down, you go up simulated hills, sprint downhill at 120 revolutions per minute, pedal in three different body positions, do jumps, and hover. Instructors call out these maneuvers choreographed to the songs in their playlist.

So why does one need a class?

Without the music, group dynamic, and dedication of talented instructors, I would not push myself nearly as hard. You burn 600-750 calories during the hour; that's about a pound a week if one makes no other changes.

Go spew some endorphins into your blood stream. Go spin.

Ordinary Hope
D.J. Christiano

Ordinary sights greeted my husband and me as we drove into the parking lot at the restaurant. I noticed weeds beginning to grow from cracks in the asphalt, an empty MacDonald's cup lying near the curb, a small pile of residual sand left over from the attempted clean-up of the winter's storms, and countless other ordinary, just ordinary, sights. We had completed another ordinary day filled with errands, household chores, etc. Even the weather was ordinary, no beautiful sunset or ominous dark clouds overhead. This had just been another day in an ordinary life.

It was my idea to go to dinner that evening. Boredom had set in. I guessed I had had enough of the ordinary. To get my husband to agree to go out, I told him he could pick the restaurant. I was sure he would choose an Italian meal. I was shocked when he said he wanted to go to the Hazel River Inn in Culpeper. We had not been there together in at least two years.

This restaurant had been the favorite meeting place for my "girls' night out." Although we were hardly girls, we had found ourselves laughing and talking and planning and hoping as if we were back in high school again. The times of fun had been replaced by life's events that we knew would happen someday. That someday came far too quickly for two of my friends. The remainder of the group soon found excuses not to see each other. I had given a few myself. I believed it was our way of self-protection; to keep the good times locked in our memories and not face the sad truths of life.

As I was getting out of the car, a huge black SUV swerved into the neighboring spot. I looked to see who the driver was, but I could barely see through the darkly tinted glass. I thought I saw the outline of a rather large man talking loudly to someone. He was obviously not in a good mood. Since I could not see another figure in the car, I assumed he was on his cell. I am not sure why this added to my anxiety about going into the restaurant, but it did.

We walked toward the familiar brick building, and my nerves seemed to have gotten the best of me. My feet felt as if they were not touching the ground. I grabbed hold of my husband's arm to steady myself and glanced back. The man in the SUV got out of his vehicle and paced back and forth as he looked at his watch. The license plate was not from Virginia. I was familiar with its white-blue color and markings. He was a New Yorker. I turned around to concentrate on my walk to the restaurant. I tried to think positive thoughts to quell my fears.

My heartbeat quickened, and I had trouble breathing. A full-blown panic attack was near. I could hardly wait to sit down; I was afraid that I would fall into a miserable heap right in the middle of the floor, embarrassing my husband, myself, and dishonoring the memories of former celebrations at the Inn. Sipping some water, I scanned the room. A couple sat in one corner, enjoying their wine; a large group was in the center, obviously celebrating a family event. Upon closer look, an elderly woman at that table wore a red-rose corsage. I guessed it was a birthday event. I tried to focus on happy times and the peacefulness and love that I shared with my family and friends.

One deep breath after another, more sips of ice water, and more deep breaths started to put things in order. I finally had the courage to look to the corner where my girls' group had sat. The staff was always accommodating, setting up tables so the eight of us would be comfortable and have a little privacy. Instead of our happy group, only one person sat in the far corner. I felt a little sorry for him. I took another sip of water.

My husband was never at a loss for a topic of conversation. Tonight I was grateful that all I had to say at intervals were short comments like, "I agree." or "That's right." My eyes drifted back to the lone man in the corner. He was rather young, mid-thirties, I guessed. He was well groomed; even his curly brown hair had been carefully brushed into place. He was very busy, pulling out one file folder after another from his briefcase. His red tie had been loosened to accommodate his determined work style. Even his white starched shirt with sleeves rolled up seemed to have had a busy day. I suspected he was an editor trying to meet a deadline, or perhaps an accountant trying to get numbers in order for an audit.

Our waitress arrived. I ordered a salad. I was feeling a bit better as I focused on the imaginary tale of the man who occupied our old corner, but I didn't want to order anything too heavy. I never quite trusted that my anxiety would be gone from minute to minute. My imaginary tale continued as I watched the man take out his cell. He looked at it repeatedly as if he expected a call or message. He must have gotten the message he was waiting for. He took his cell, picked up a folder and walked quickly outside. His blue jacket fell off his chair and onto the floor.

I thought about telling him about his jacket as he walked past our table. The look on his face told me he would not find that as important as what he was doing. I heard his shoes squeak as he hurried to the door, and so did my husband, who commented about how good leather shoes always squeak when they are new. I now decided that the busy man was probably an attorney, gathering information for a pending trial. Maybe a University of Virginia grad with tan pants, blue jacket and all. No, the red tie did not fit into the UVA garb.

The waitress arrived at the man's table with his dinner. I couldn't tell what he had ordered and didn't want to stare more than I already had. I was surprised when my supposed attorney walked in with the man who had hastily arrived in the SUV. When the "attorney" sat down and looked through another folder, I got a closer look at the mystery man who drove SUV. He was rather large with a black suit and white shirt, no tie. I now knew why he chose the comfort of the SUV. His round face nervously looked around at the door several times while the attorney looked in a few more folders. At one point, the SUV man and I made eye contact. I quickly turned away. The two had a quick exchange of words, and the SUV man exited, walking briskly, his eyes focused straight ahead while mine strayed back to the corner table. I was more engrossed in the young "attorney's" tale than I was with my current situation.

Our dinner arrived in a few minutes. I even felt somewhat hungry. I glanced every so often at the corner table; everything had returned to something very ordinary. I thought to myself that I must indeed have a strange mind. I could not believe the mysterious story I had just made up to protect myself from reality. Time passed pleasantly as we finished our meal. My focus was on dinner and our current conversation. As my husband paid the bill, I held my wine glass up for a short toast to past memories and vowed to get in touch with remaining friends. Maybe they would be ready to resume our girls' nights.

As we walked back to the parking lot, I saw something lying on the ground. I thought at first someone dropped a blue coat, but when I looked closer, I saw it was the handsome young man. Had he stumbled and hit his head? I pointed in the direction of the man and told my husband as calmly as I could about what I saw.

We both ran to see if we could help.

As I ran, I yelled out, "Are you okay?" No answer. I know just as much about emergency medicine as you learn from TV. Never move anyone who is unconscious. Neither one of us touched the man, but we did notice there was blood on his right temple. I quickly assumed that he had fallen. We had to get him some help. I looked quickly around. No one was in sight. As I walked into the street, I did see a County Sheriff car driving toward us. I waved my hands; the car started moving quicker and stopped. I directed the officer to the accident. My head was swimming in a sea of anxiety, fear, and worry.

Out of the corner of my eye, I saw a black shape walking calmly down the street with a briefcase. I thought to myself, I know that figure. I did not turn to verify my suspicion. I stood frozen in place. My conscious told me to yell out to the officer, "Arrest that guy!" Self-preservation kept me silent.

An ambulance soon came with lights flashing and a short burst of a siren. The officer came over to get our names and asked us for any information we could give him. At that moment, I had to decide how much of what I saw I would share.

As the ambulance pulled away, I hoped and prayed the man would be okay. I told the officer that I saw the man eating dinner alone and about his visitor. The rest would have to wait for another day. I secretly hoped that all would be resolved before I had to make a decision. I hoped my memory would forget the specific letters and numbers on the license plate. As the ambulance door closed, I heard moans coming from the victim. I had a feeling that he would be fine and safe for at least the evening. I also knew that when I got home, my phone call to the police would include the license plate information. I then hoped for an ordinary day tomorrow.

An Atypical Tuesday

Diane Burdette

Shake, rattle, and roll may sound like the lyrics to an old song, but for me, these words describe the earthquake that recently passed through our area. August 23, 2011, started out like a typical Tuesday, but at 1:55 in the afternoon, everything changed. While I was stacking dishes in my cabinets, a low, rumbling noise began. Within seconds the sound had accelerated. All of the dishes started to rattle, and the whole house began to shake. I glanced above to see if the ceiling was still intact, then quickly ran outside. Standing on the pavement, I felt as though the ground was rolling beneath my feet. Stunned and confused, I remained there until all of the vibrations had subsided.

As I had suspected, a major earthquake had struck Virginia. It had a magnitude of 5.8 on the Richter scale. The last quake of this proportion in our state was 114 years ago. Many people along the East Coast experienced the tremors, and some structures were damaged.

Scientists seem to think this was the quake of our century. I hope they are right, for the shake, rattle, and roll of this one was enough for me!

My Lunch Date in Charlottesville

MaryAnn Morrison

I was looking forward to my lunch date with Punky in Charlottesville. I live in Locust Grove, but I could get lost in my own backyard. I had purchased a GPS and called it Mumzie because of its female voice. God bless the inventor of the GPS; it got me safely to my destination.

Many years ago, Punky and I had met at Plymouth State Teachers College in New Hampshire, now a university. Some of us were transfer students. The regular dorm rooms were full. I found myself in the basement floor with eight girls and three rooms. They were the last rooms available, and we felt lucky to have them to ourselves for one year. In those three rooms, the eight of us formed a sisterhood. We had our ups and downs as we were growing together to become women. We still try to get together for lunch once a month.

At lunch Punky and I discussed the state of the union, young people, cell phones, television, teachers, and drugs. I confessed that I am often frustrated because I miss the operator who knew everyone in town, and modern television shows overwhelm me. I admitted that I frequently tune into the Hallmark channel when I need a break.

Punky and her husband Ken had just returned from Holland and Turkey, and she had 300 wonderful pictures. Even though they missed the tulip season by one week, there was still plenty to see. The architecture of the centuries-old buildings was mesmerizing, strong, connected and well cared for.

After lunch we lingered in the stores and appreciated the artwork displays. We parted, and I headed back to Locust Grove. As I drove, I saw Yard Sale signs dotting the roads like advertisements. When I saw the displays, I noticed no one was buying.

Along this road were mansions that sat tall and straight overlooking the land. They had survived for hundreds of years. The scenery was beautiful with spring blooms enjoying their time in the sun. 'Mumzie' was still taking good care of me so I didn't get lost once.

The sign for Orange beckoned. I decided to ignore my GPS and followed the arrow pointing left. Orange is a cute little village. I stopped at a roadside stand. While I was waiting to make my purchase, I learned that the owner of the stand was responsible for the homemade goodies and fresh eggs. One customer bought goods while her elderly mother waited in the car. A young man picked up three loaves of bread he had ordered the day before. I couldn't ignore the tables that held such alluring treats. I bought several of the delightful pastries and started eating them before I even got back to the car.

My next stop was Gypsy Willow, a quiet place that sells period clothes and other items. You might find that beautiful set of china you have always wanted, and the prices are reasonable. Tara is the owner. She gives all the help you need and none of the pressure often found in other shops. Gypsy Willow is a perfect name for Tara's shop. It reflects her personality, uniquely gentle, like a willow in the wind.

I had parked my car across the street near an abandoned building. It seemed like a perfect parking place. It had an old U-turn driveway, probably four or five feet high at its center. I could envision a beautiful garden in that circular space that now held water, weeds, and other things less visible. After browsing in Gypsy Willow, I gave Tara a wave and headed for my car.

I buckled my seatbelt and started the car. I turned the wheels to the right to descend the curved driveway. The minute I stepped on the gas, the car and I started to turn over. Had it not been for the metal bar that formed an arch for the driveway, the car and I would have landed upside down on the street. I got out of the car to take a look.

I confess I was a bit shaken. Before I could do anything, a lady in a truck slammed on her brakes. She and two men who were accompanying her were the first ones on the scene. They started yelling, "Don't call for help. Really, don't. Save your money. We can pick it up ourselves." Today I wouldn't be able to describe any of those people, but I did notice that the woman was wearing a red-flannel shirt.

It was plain to see my 1998 Honda was being held by its front bumper on that metal arch. My bumper now had a dent in the middle, and the right front tire was suspended in space.

"Get in the car," Red commanded. "When I say 'ready,' we are going to pick the car up and push it backwards."

"You can't stand in front of the car. What if it falls on someone?" I gasped, horrified.

By this time, we were gathering onlookers and one more helper. When a truck came by, Red told the driver, "Get over here. Help us. It's the right thing to do." I could see Red was a take-charge lady.

I was directed to get in the car, put it in reverse, and when given the word, I was to press on the gas. I was so afraid I would do the wrong thing and kill them all. I pleaded with one of the men to do it for me, but he said, "I can't. You aren't strong enough to lift." I certainly couldn't argue with that.

That man did slip, and almost fell. My heart was racing so fast. I wanted to stop, but he quickly found his footing, and I heard Red yell, "*Now!*" I stepped on the gas, backed up and finally felt myself settled on the driveway.

Red and her boys had done the job and had already turned around to leave. My vehicle was freed, and no one was dead. I was so grateful and relieved I ran over to Red and gave her a big hug. The tears started running down my face. I hugged her and cried until she hugged me back. After I hugged all of them, Red and her boys were half-way across the street heading for their truck. I didn't even learn any names. I called her Red because of her red shirt, or was the truck red? I'm not sure which, perhaps both.

Not knowing their names, however, didn't stop me from clearly knowing their hearts. I know they are not people who would expect or accept payment for their good works. Their truths in life are simple: "If you can help someone, do it. It's the right thing to do." I was reminded of my own parents who shared the same philosophy and taught it to their three children.

My mother always wanted to travel across the country, but she was too busy taking care of others. I called her Mumzie, also. I take her spirit with me wherever I go. She would have been pleased that people still do the "right thing."

I know that people make choices every minute of each day; those choices are the building blocks of what and who they become as individuals. My tears of loving gratitude touched all their faces.

I can't promise I'll hold a car up for someone, but 'Mumzie' and I promise to repay the kindness going forward. Remember, if you can help someone, do it. It's the right thing to do. Thanks Red.

A Look Into the Past
Caryn Moya Block

It has always amazed me how reading can change your life. I am a voracious reader. I love to lose myself in a good book. But I wasn't always fond of reading.

As a child, even before starting school, my mother would read to my brother and me. One of my favorite stories, and one I still have in my library today, was *Winnie the Pooh* by A.A. Milne. My mother bought it for me at Disneyland on my fourth birthday. I loved snuggling down to listen to her read to us.

My father's mother also liked to spoil me by buying beautifully illustrated fairytale books with ladies in gorgeous gowns and knights in shining armor.

Once I started reading in school, I struggled with Dick and Jane until my mother bought me my first Nancy Drew mystery written by Carolyn Keene. Then I was hooked and as the saying goes "She was off..."

I continued to read Nancy Drew until I finished the whole series and then advanced to the Hardy Boys by Franklin W. Dixon and other mysteries. When I started middle school, I had graduated to Sherlock Holmes by Arthur Conan Doyle and Agatha Christie's Miss Marple mysteries. I also read all the horse and dog books that I could get my hands on, like *My Friend Flika* by Mary O'Hara, *Big Red*, and *Lassie*.

In high school I started to read fantasy and science fiction. My favorite authors were Andre Norton, Anne McCaffrey, and Mercedes Lackey. *Cat's Eyes* was my favorite novel. These books were full of psychic powers and talking animals. I also read the Merlin stories by Mary Stewart, and, another favorite, *The Three Musketeers* by Alexandre Dumas.

But wait, you might ask, where are the Romance books? Well . . . I have to say I am a late comer to the romance genre. Not that there wasn't a lot of romance in the books I read. They just weren't labeled as such.

Many years after college graduation, a friend suggested I try a medieval romance book. Knowing I was guaranteed a happy ending during a difficult time in my life, I decided to go for it. And I was hooked. I still read an occasional sci-fi book or mystery, but my heart now belongs to the romance genre.

If you know any of the books I've mentioned, you can almost make out the road map to the author I have become. I write paranormal romance books with men who turn into wolves and have a psychic bond with their mates. Can you see the road signs? What are the books you have read that show the world the person you have become?

Drawing: © Dina Buckley

The Easter Suit
Lois Powell

Auntie Mable always gave us our Easter outfits. This year she gave Hargrave a suit that was his pride and joy. It made him feel like a man, like Daddy, even though he was only eight and in the third grade. It was his first suit with long pants. It was a brown glen-plaid wool with a three-button jacket. He also had a white long-sleeve shirt and red-striped tie. He wore the outfit to Sunday School every week, no matter how many times Mommy tried to get him to wear something else for a change.

When we came home from Sunday School, my sister Pat and I would change our clothes, but not Hargrave. He'd wear that suit all day. No one could get him to take it off.

This particular Sunday was cloudy and glum outside. Pat, Hargrave and I were upstairs in the bedroom, playing around, not doing anything special. Mommy called upstairs.

"Why don't you all go to the movies. It's a great day to go since it's so gloomy outside."

We thought about it for a hot second and decided: Why not? There's nothing else to do.

"Okay! We'll go," said Pat. Pat was the oldest. She was in eighth grade and usually would rather be with her friends than with us. I was in fifth grade.

"Hargrave, change that suit before you go. I don't want you getting it all dirty," said Mommy.

Hargrave hung his head and pouted his mouth and looked at us with his sad puppy-dog eyes. Then, raising his head and eyebrows, he ran to the top of the stairs.

"Gee Mommy, do I have ta? I promise I'll be real careful and not get anything on it. Please Mommy. I promise, cross my throat and hope to choke," pleaded Hargrave.

Usually pleading or begging with Mommy didn't mean a thing, but for some reason she let him keep it on.

"Okay! But you better be careful. If anything happens to that suit, you'll be in big trouble," said Mommy.

Hargrave ran downstairs, and we followed. He gave Mommy a huge hug. Mommy and Daddy were sitting in the living room reading the newspaper. Daddy shook his head and laughed.

"I hope you won't have to choke," said Daddy.

Mommy went and got the money and gave it to Pat.

"There's enough money so you can buy popcorn or a candy bar. Pat, make sure all of you stay together," said Mommy, giving Pat that Mother look.

"Thanks, and we will," said Pat.

We were off. We walked the three blocks to the bus stop and caught the bus to go downtown. At that time we were still living in New Haven, Connecticut. We never noticed the sun was hiding behind the clouds.

By the time the movie was over, it was dark outside. Pat made us all hold hands as we walked to the bus stop, which was only a block away from the theater. While we waited, the sky just opened up, and it started pouring. It was as if someone opened a fire hydrant. When the bus came, we quickly jumped on it. We all huddled into one seat to get warm. We couldn't stop shivering. Hargrave was between us. He looked at me and then Pat and started crying. I should say hollering. Pat put her arm around him, and I held his hand.

"Mommy is going to kill me. I promised nothing would happen to my Easter suit and now it's all wet," cried Hargrave.

"Don't cry Hargrave. Mommy will understand. No one knew it was going to rain," said Pat, trying to console him.

But he kept crying, and I kept rubbing his hand. When we were almost home, I noticed that Hargrave's sleeve looked shorter. Or was it my imagination? I grabbed his other hand, and that sleeve looked shorter too.

"Pat, do Hargrave's sleeves look shorter to you?" I asked.

She looked, and her eyes got wide. We could actually see his suit shrinking. The pant legs were getting shorter, too. Pat and I tried to pull the material down, but our efforts didn't help. They made Hargrave cry even more. He looked so funny. Pat and I glanced at one another and tried not to laugh. I could feel the giggle in the pit of my belly.

By the time we got off the bus and looked at the suit, we noticed that the sleeves and pant legs were at least two inches shorter. It was still raining so we ran home as fast as we could. When we arrived, we yanked open the door and burst into the hallway. Mommy and Daddy came running. They had on their rain coats.

"We were just leaving to pick you up. We weren't sure when the movie would be over," said Daddy.

Hargrave took one look at them and started bawling again. Daddy gave him a hug and brought him into the living room with us following. Mommy went to get towels for us. Daddy sat down in his favorite chair with Hargrave facing him. Placing his hands on Hargrave's shoulders, he was getting ready to say something when he took a good look at Hargrave. The suit had shrunk even more. Daddy sat there with his mouth hanging open, just staring.

Mommy came back into the living room and handed us our towels when she realized we were all staring at Hargrave. She looked too.

"Oh my God! What happened to your suit?" asked Mommy.

Pat blurted out, "It shrunk."

The giggle rolled up to my throat. Pat and I couldn't hold it any longer. We burst out laughing and couldn't stop. Mommy and Daddy tried to make us stop, but it didn't work. We all looked at poor drenched Hargrave in the shrinking suit. Daddy picked him up and put him on his lap. He put his arms around him, trying to make him feel better, but it didn't help. Hargrave just kept on bawling.

Hargrave is now sixty-plus years old and a successful lawyer with his own firm. We still retell the story every Easter when we're together. He doesn't cry about the suit anymore but laughs with the rest of us and says, "Check out my suits now."

Miracle Worker

Gwen Monohan

She visited every day
the old folks
in The Home.
Carried their trays.
Helped them eat.
Dispensed sweet treats.
And read to them
verses from the *Bible*
or *Huckleberry Finn*.

She worked hours at
a time, finding ways
to make their stays
more meaningful.
Her own bone cancer is
in remission now.
Tumors have shrunk.
It's a miraculous cure,
Her doctors say.

A Blue Screen Chat

Jack Daily

Lisa leaned back in her chair and spoke to the blue screen. "You never work when it matters most. I dust your keys, I clean your registry, I get you updates on time. Why aren't you more friendly?"

She had just lost the last hour of work in Word. It was the final edit of the book's last chapter. The one that was due tomorrow.

The monitor stared back but remained quiet.

"I knew I should have backed up. I knew it, I knew it, I knew it."

Lisa got up from the chair, walked into the small living room and lay down on the couch. Two minutes later, she stood up and shouted, "I hate those friggin' *Life Is Good* T-shirts."

She went back into the bedroom where the computer comfortably sat. The blue screen seemed to shine more brightly. Lisa opened the bottom drawer of her chest and pulled out a T-shirt. It was aqua and, in pink letters, said *Life is Good*.

She held the shirt in front of her, arms outstretched, turned toward the computer, and said, "I want you to watch something."

Lisa reached over to the pen receptacle on her desk, withdrew the scissors, and began to cut the T-shirt in half.

She smiled at the monitor and asked, "Did you see that?"

The monitor gave an almost imperceptible blink.

Lisa threw the scissors back on the desk, tossed the top half of the shirt on her bed and kicked the other half to the corner of the bedroom. She eased back into her desk chair, moved in closer to the monitor and defiantly said, "I've been thinking about this for a while. I'm buying a Mac."

The monitor said nothing and seemed not to care.

In Her Words

*Women's stories, funny
and poignant, come from
the heart of life.*

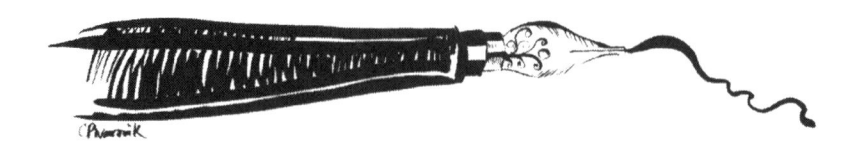

Drawing: © Carole Pivarnik

A Writer's Dream
Ruby E. Pruit

Ink on thumb,

Pen in hand,

Now if I could just overcome this writer's block,

While I can still find my pen!

The Yard Sale

Lavanda Woodall

I'd best tell you right up front that I look on goin' to yard and garage sales as a sport, kindly like tennis or golf maybe, but a whole lot more fun.

The best yard sale I ever went to was on a Saturday mornin' about a year ago. Me and everybody else around here always looked forward to the first Saturday in June when Lula Mae Brown held her annual yard sale. She'd have a table set up with coffee and sweet rolls, or maybe a cake or two. You could always count on it.

She'd usually make good on her sale, too. I knowed Lula Mae had to do all kinds of things to make money 'cause her husband Arnold wasn't what you'd call real work brittle. In fact, the man wouldn't hit a lick at a snake if it was about to bite him. Oh, he did have jobs on occasion. I know there was the time somebody got Arnold a job on the railroad. About six weeks after Arnold went to work, his boss Harley Simmons came draggin' him home. Harley was cussin' and hollerin' somethin' terrible.

"Lula Mae," he yelled, "you keep this dumb excuse for a human bein' away from my railroad!"

Now, if Arnold did have one besettin' sin, it was he had to know about everything. How? Why? Where, and so on. Somebody over to the railroad told Arnold that whatever he did, don't pull that big red switch down by the old depot, but they never told him why. Well sir, the idea of that switch just ate on Arnold 'til he couldn't stand it anymore, and one day he just up and yanked it back for all he was worth. Somebody seen him do it and, just in the nick of time, pulled it back in place. Turned out that the switch would have let a passenger train that was on the main track run onto a sidin' where the railroad stored several freight cars full of dynamite. Arnold's curiosity almost blowed up the south end of Cade County.

When I got to the sale (my third of the day), I could see that there was a lot of folks already there. I parked my car and set out on foot. Not bein' overly blessed with height, I couldn't see squat over all the people crowded in Lula Mae's front yard. Finally, with a little pushin' and shovin', I made it up front.

Well, sir, there stood Lula Mae and Sheriff Dan Murphy faced off in Lula Mae's driveway. Over to one side a little bit was a big high-back chair. And settin' in the chair was Arnold Brown. The man was dressed fit-to-kill in his best suit. Bow tie. Shiny shoes, and all. And hangin' around his neck was a hand-painted sign that said: FOR SALE.

Well! I knowed that Lula Mae was fed up to her ears with old Arnold, but who'da thought she'd go so far as to sell him! On the driveway beside Arnold was his old huntin' dog, Beauregard, and a couple of beat-up suitcases. There wasn't a doubt in my mind that the suitcases was full of Arnold's clothes and stuff. It looked like Lula Mae was goin' for a clean slate.

Sudie Powell had her hand in the air. "I'll buy him! I need a handy man to do odd jobs around my place!"

Arnold was odd, I'll say that for him, but Sudie'd best look somewhere else 'cause the feller was about as handy as a wart on a hawg.

The sheriff gave Lula Mae a straight look. "Miz Lula Mae, you can't sell your husband. It's against the law."

"What law?" Lula Mae looked like one of them pug dogs.

"I don't know right off. I just know it's against the law to sell people. Besides, nobody would buy the old buzzard!"

Well, I don't know about that. There's several folks around here dumb enough to buy a buzzard.

Then, Myrtle Reed went over and checked out Arnold's teeth. I knowed Myrtle had been on the lookout for years for somebody to warm her toes. From lookin' at Arnold, though, I didn't think he was up for much toe-warmin'.

"Well, I'm goin' to get shet of him one way or another. I've had a belly full of caps off the toothpaste, and toilet seats left up so when a body sets down, it's farther than you think!" By that time, Lula Mae was foamin' at the mouth. In my opinion, the woman appeared to be livin' on the business end of a short fuse.

About that time, Deputy Gluford Boggs showed up. Sticky, as we all called him, started talkin' to the sheriff. They both glanced over at Arnold, and I wondered if they was rememberin' the time when Arnold was a deputy sheriff. That job didn't last long either.

It musta been in the spring, 'cause it was still cool at night. It all happened when a couple of Yankee bank robbers came through Cades Ridge and robbed the 13th National Bank and the Fruit and Vegetable Pickers Savings and Loan Association. Monroe Jenkins and Eugene Barker, the robbers, stood at seven and eight on the FBI's most-wanted list. Ada Sue Reeves, who worked at the bank, pushed the alarm button under her desk. It was real unfortunate that Sticky Boggs and his new partner Arnold Brown answered the summons. The Cade County deputies caught up with the bank robbers about five miles outside of town, where Barker and Jenkins ran the police car off the road. After a short gun battle, Arnold managed to shoot hisself in the foot.

Anyway, the upshot of it was that the two robbers took the police car and left Arnold and Sticky (naked as jaybirds) handcuffed together around a good-size tree.

It musta been four days later when Barker and Jenkins was finally captured while tryin' to rob a pet store outside of Atlanter. When they was questioned by the FBI as to what they did with the two deputies from Cade County, Monroe Jenkins admitted that him and Eugene Barker had wanted to kill the two cops, but just couldn't quite bring theirselves to pull the trigger. As Monroe told one agent, "Those two had to be the sorriest law enforcement officers we ever run across and, well, we just couldn't do it."

It was just too bad that before the FBI could let Sheriff Murphy know his men was still alive, a troop of Girl Scouts, on their yearly spring hike, came across Arnold and Sticky still hangin' onto the tree. Berle Ames, who was leadin' the scouts, told the Cades Ridge Tribune Examiner that it was a sight to behold. She said the girls, after takin' a good look at the naked deputies, screamed and run off in every direction.

Doc Henry Bean told me that the flies and mosquitoes had come within an ace of eatin' the men alive. They was both sufferin' from exposure, and by that time Arnold's foot was infected real bad.

After a week in the hospital, Arnold quit the police force. Said he believed it was more than he could handle. That's probably true.

Listenin' to all the ruckus at the yard sale had give me a real appetite, so I moseyed over to the refreshment table before all the food was gone.

About that time, a big van drove up, and a bunch of women piled out. They was big. Real big, and tall. And they all looked mean and hard as nails.

"Hey Lula Mae," the biggest one bellered, "I'm here to buy your man for one of my girls!"

Poor Arnold turned three shades of sick and dived under the front porch. Then that idiot dog Beauregard went around Arnold's chair and started pointin' at the porch. You know, I never did like that dog after he went naughty on my boots a couple of winters ago.

By some miracle, I was the only one who seen where Arnold disappeared to. When the feller couldn't be found, the yard sale kindly went to pot.

Anyway, I don't know what went on at the Brown's house after everybody left, but the next week Lula Mae bought Arnold one of them big ridin' mowers. And Arnold started mowin' all over town. Seven days a week. It was clear that he had the bejabbers scared out of him. Even though he is mowin' grass all the time, I hope he's not still leavin' caps off the toothpaste and such as that. It wouldn't take all that much to set Lula Mae off, and I'm afraid that next time, Arnold will find hisself warmin' toes for one of them great big gals.

Tomorrow Is on Hold

Bobbie Troy

Tomorrow Is on Hold. That was the headline news in all the media. The Senatorial Committee usually made its decision by 6:00 p.m. Eastern Standard Time (EST), but today it was delayed. As agreed by this committee of three persons, there could be only two reasons for not approving tomorrow: (1) an impending nuclear disaster, which would make it futile to have another day, or (2) a two-thirds majority of the country's citizens did not vote for another day by 5:00 p.m. EST on www.voteyestomorrow.com. Since most people wanted to live another day, the second reason was usually not a problem. So the logical deduction was an impending nuclear disaster. But still the people waited and waited and hoped and hoped that tomorrow would be approved by 6:00 p.m.

Son Leaving for College
Martha Orr Conn

I saw

His trunk

Go out the door,

And boxes

And cartons

By the score.

How come his room

Still holds

So much more?

Ladies' Man

Lavanda Woodall

John Jones was what we used to call a Ladies' Man. He'd bless you with that sweet smile of hisn', and every female from six to sixty would melt right where they was standin'.

John had no looks to speak of. Well, I'll just tell you plain out like, that the boy was homely enough to make a freight train take a dirt road.

I always wondered what John's big attraction was, but bein' a church-goin' maiden lady, I wasn't curious enough to find out first hand, you understand.

John had been married to Tess for close to thirty years. I know the woman was upset over John's tomcattin' around the way he did, but every time it happened, Tess would make excuses for him. You never in your life heard so many reasons why John did it. One time I heard Tess say that John needed more than she could give him. More what? Then several years ago, she told me that she wasn't the easiest person to get along with. Last year, she told somebody else that John was a little on the dumb side. Well, I never heard of dumb bein' an excuse for such as that. But you know, he coulda been dumb. When John wasn't smilin', his face always did have a blank look about it. In fact, every time I saw him, I wanted to knock on his head and ask, "Is anybody in there?" I reckon him and Tess was about even on that score 'cause she sure didn't have a monopoly on smarts, either.

Anyway, Tess would make excuses for John, then she'd threaten to sew up his pants. John would promise to stay home, but the next thing you know, John was seein' this one or runnin' around with that one.

John wasn't any too fussy in who he bestowed his favors on, neither. Some was young. Others wasn't. Some was pretty. Some not. Didn't make a particle of difference. John seemed to love 'em all.

Tess and John never had any young'uns. That ain't to say that John never had any kids. He did. All over Cade County. Bea Jefferson's oldest was John's boy, and everybody knowed that at least two of Annie Booth's eight had John Jones writ all over 'em. Then, too, if I wasn't mistaken, Reedie Mumford's last child was the spittin' image of John.

I'd like to tell you right here that none of the husbands of "John's Ladies," as we called 'em, pitched a fit at havin' a cuckoo in his nest. If I'da been Lonnie Jefferson or Gilbert Booth, I'da beat the livin' tar outta John Jones and kicked my wife outta the house. I can't for the life of me figure out why they put up with it. Oh well, it takes all kinds.

When you talk with Tess Jones, she was always somewhere between snippy and snarly. I never was real sure whether her aptitude was because of John's tomcattin', or John ran around 'cause he didn't want to listen to Tess rant and rave. In this case, I think cause and effect was bitin' each other on the rear end. Wonder why John and Tess stayed together? It could be that they was used to each other. Seems like some marriages are like that. Maybe it's a case of the devil you know.

John told me one time that he'd like to travel. I heard him say that he'd like to go to Florida. Then, he talked about Californey. A couple other times I heard him mention other places he'd like to visit. John never made much money, and Tess never worked outside the home. So I reckon there wasn't enough money to do any travelin'. Why didn't John just take off by hisself to see the world? It looked like to me that the only roamin' John did was from woman to woman and bed to bed.

In Her Words

Another thing I'd really wanted to know was when exactly John had the time to run around. I'd see him leave his house about seven every mornin' and get home around four in the afternoon.

Turned out that John was in the habit of takin' some real long lunch breaks. He'd leave work at eleven or so and get back at one or two in the afternoon. A body could get all over Cade County inside of two hours. Looked like John could and did.

Things just went on in the same old way 'til John up and died. Tess had this great big funeral at the Come All Sinners Baptist Church and buried him in a fancy silver-lookin' casket.

Tess took John's dyin' somethin' fierce. The woman cried and carried on 'til we was all fed up with it. It looked to me that John was a whole lot less trouble dead than he was alive. Good Grief! You'd think she'd be relieved at knowin' where the old goat was all the time! But no, I'd see Tess over there at the cemetery behind the Baptist church puttin' flowers on John's grave and cryin' up a storm.

Tess had just quieted down about a year ago, when it started rainin'. Well, sir, it rained from about the middle of April 'til sometime in July. On the fourth of July, it was still rainin' cats and dogs. A bunch of us was standin' alongside Main Street with our umbrellies watchin' the American Legion parade go by. Right before the Cade County fire truck passed us, we heard this terrible loud noise. Everybody ran over to the other side of the street to see what was goin' on.

Now, the Come All Sinners Baptist Church Cemetery was on real low-lyin' ground, and runnin' alongside the graveyard was Big Tilden Creek.

I couldn't believe what I was seein'! Right before my eyes a big chunk of ground broke off the cemetery and out floated this silver casket. There it was bobbin' along in the churnin' flood waters and then all of a sudden, it turned and headed downstream.

Somebody said, "Oh my Lord, ain't that John Jones' casket?"

Tess Jones was standin' right next to me. I couldn't help lookin' at her to see how she was takin' John's sudden bolt for freedom.

Tess stared at the silver casket, then said, "Well, John always did want to travel."

We all turned to look at her. One last excuse, I thought.

There was a big crack from the cemetery and another section of ground fell away. Two more caskets floated out.

Then, Lydia Carter started jumpin' up and down. "I think that pinkish lookin' coffin belongs to Gracie Linder."

Archie Doolittle pointed at the other one and said it was more than likely Faye Meecham's.

Well sir, it appeared like John Jones was finally leavin' town, and he wasn't goin' alone.

Drawing: © Arlene Baker

Woman on the Porch

Bobbie Troy

The first time we passed the house, I barely noticed it because it was set back from the road and weathered enough so that the gray blended in with early evening sky. The next time, I was with my friend Diane, and she asked me if I knew that the house was haunted.

Yeah, right. I don't think so.

It is. It really is. The ghost of an old woman comes out at night and sweeps the porch. Then she disappears.

Well, I don't believe you, and I'm not afraid of passing that house any time of the day or night. And I'll accept that dare you were about to throw my way. I'll watch the house from 9 p.m. on. If the old lady doesn't come out by midnight, I'll run up on the porch and bang on the door and see what happens.

§ § §

Well, said Diane, what happened last night? You must have froze your butt off. It was really cold out there.

Frozen and scared, that's what I was. Nothing happened until about 11:00 p.m. Then I saw a faint light on the porch that just appeared suddenly. Then something or someone was moving back and forth, back and forth. I couldn't make out what was really going on, though. But a slight breeze suddenly came up, and I hightailed it outta' there.

Well, do you believe me now?

Yeah, I sure do, I said.

§ § §

Early the next morning, Diane went by the house and made sure that her bag with the makeup and wig was still under the porch. Then she grabbed it and ran, hoping that nobody saw her. As for the broom, it could stay there until next time.

Unlikely Fantasy

Martha Orr Conn

I've been to the grocery,
Brought the bags home,
And emptied them all of their lot.

I've fridged all the fresh stuff,
Spun out the greens,
And didn't think of one thing I forgot.

Oh, would that it were so!

Second-Story Man

Lavanda Woodall

It musta been about ten years ago when my nephew Alfred took up bein' a thief. Alfred, Al for short, wasn't what you'd call a bad child. Just not real bright.

After Al graduated from high school, he went off to the state university. The poor feller didn't last two months over there til he got sent home. He said there wasn't enough money for college, but the truth of the matter was that Alfred couldn't figure out how to sign up for his classes.

Right after Al got home, he got a job at Bickel's grocery store. Stockin' shelves, moppin' floors, and doin' whatever needed to be done around the place.

Five years later, Alfred was still at the store. Workin' at the same old job. Stockin' shelves and moppin' floors. It was a dead-end job that didn't pay all that much money.

I reckon Alfred got to feelin' that things was passin' him by. Which they was. So the boy tried to come up with how to change his life and make a tad more money in the process. Finally, after a lot of cogitatin' Al decided to become a second-story man. If he couldn't work for it, he'd steal it.

How people think has always been a mystery to me, and Alfred wasn't no different.

The first night Al took to thievin', he didn't have much trouble and came home with twenty-five dollars. He coulda took more. After all, there was almost a hundred dollars in Len Beeler's cookie jar. But Al wasn't greedy. He just needed a little extra cash.

The second night out, he got thirty-four dollars and twenty-eight cents. All in pennies. He also took a six-pack of beer that was settin' on the counter. Alfred didn't drink beer but decided that since he was a thief, he might take up drinkin' too.

The next Friday evenin', he tried the Watson house. Accordin' to all the stories Alfred had been told, old Miz Watson had lots of money stashed away somewhere.

Tiptoein' down a hall in the Watson house, Al passed an open doorway. A soft voice said, "Alfred, would you bring me a glass of juice before you leave?"

Alfred told me later that he came within an ace of jumpin' outta his skin. After he got his wits together, he croaked out, "Yes ma'am." Looked like poor Miz Watson was home sick in bed.

When Al looked in the refrigerator for juice, there wasn't hardly any food in there atall. Maybe Miz Watson didn't have as much money as everybody said she did.

Well sir, before he left, Al spent twenty dollars of his own money on food (good thing he'd got paid that day), heated Miz Watson some chicken soup, and walked her little dog Hoover around the block twice.

It was on Sunday night that Alfred climbed the big maple tree in the Tucker's backyard. After sneakin' through an open winder, Al tripped over a small table. It was just unfortunate that when Alfred lost his footin', he fell right on top of Bebe Tucker. Bebe, whose husband, Norbert, was out of town for a week, kept poor Alfred in that bedroom for the next three days. Al liked to have lost his day job at Bickel's grocery store over all that. He wasn't hurtin' for money, though, 'cause Bebe slipped him a fifty dollar bill before he left.

After that little set-to, Alfred was a tad leery about goin' out again. He sure didn't want to run into anybody like Bebe Tucker any time soon.

Sunday night Al stayed home and tried to figure out where he stood as far as the take from the part-time work. As best he could see, he was ahead by some eighty-nine dollars and twenty-eight cents. And a six-pack of beer.

After some thought, Al decided to give it one more shot, so to speak. Next weekend was the annual Fall Festival over to the Enlightened Resurrection and Life Everlastin' Catholic Church.

Everybody and his brother was likely to attend the festival 'cause the main attraction was goin' to be bingo.

Alfred thought real hard about his last go at stealin'. Maybe he'd try the Martin ladies' house. Effie and Bertha Martin was two old-maid sisters that lived over on South Elm Street. Besides, he'd always wanted to see the inside of that big place.

This time, he just walked in the back door. In the kitchen there was dirty plates on the table. It looked like the Martin sisters left in a hurry. Bingo takes some folks like that.

Al spent a good hour lookin' over the big house. There was lots of antiques scattered around the rooms, and a whole lot of pictures on nearly every wall. He even sat down with his flashlight and looked through a couple of old phonograph albums. Alfred chuckled. People sure did used to dress funny.

Later, Al found five dollars in Miz Effie's red jacket hangin' by the back door, and there was another ten on Miz Bertha's chest of drawers. Al also took what looked like an old jewelry box off the livin' room mantle. Walkin' through the dark house, Alfred accidentally stepped on Miz Bertha's ill-tempered cat Oscar. Oscar went one way, and Alfred and the box went the other. When Al switched on the kitchen light, he saw to his horror that the box had been full of ashes. Unknown to Alfred, the Martin sisters had kept the ashes of their daddy, Thomas Scully Martin, on the mantelpiece in the livin' room. It took Al a minute or two to find a broom and dust pan. Now, the Martins hadn't had time to sweep the kitchen that day, so when Alfred swept up the ashes, he got peas, pieces of cereal, and a lone radish from lunch. Al just dumped the whole mess in the small wood box. After puttin' the box in a small bag, the boy took off for home as fast as he could go.

Poor Alfred. There he was with about a hundred dollars or so for several weeks' work. And he still had the six-pack of beer and Thomas Martin's ashes. It wasn't as much fun bein' a thief as he thought it would be. Alfred was real unhappy about the way the whole thing had turned out. It was really more than he could deal with, so Monday after work he went to see Sheriff Dan Murphy and turned hisself in.

Alfred told the sheriff the whole story from start to finish. Stealin' pennies. Miz Watson's juice. Climbin' through winders. Bebe Tucker. Ashes. The whole works.

Dan told me later that when Alfred got to the part about sweepin' up Thomas Martin's ashes, he almost hurrawed right in the boy's face.

Finally it was quiet. And after watchin' Al fidget for a while, Dan said, "What do you think ought to happen here, Alfred?"

"I don't know, Sheriff. But somehow I've got to give the money back to all those folks." By that time, Alfred was sweatin' real good.

"How are you goin' to do that?"

"Sneak back in with it?" Alfred said.

Dan snorted. "You were real lucky you didn't get caught takin' it out. No sayin' what would happen if you tried to take it back. No sir, that's not gonna work twice. I've got to give this some thought." Dan gave the boy a real hard look. "I believe I can keep you out of jail, Alfred, but you're not gettin' off scot free. I'll tell you what. Before you leave here, go in the back room there and pick all that cereal and peas and stuff out of those ashes, and then we'll take old Thomas home."

Dan said when Alfred came outta that back room, he looked sick as a dog.

When they got to the Martin house, Dan called Effie and Bertha out in their front yard while Alfred put the wood box back on the livin' room mantle. He also stuck fifteen dollars in the pocket of Effie's red jacket.

The next week Dan told Alfred to give the rest of the money to the Red Cross. And all the next winter, Alfred volunteered his time around town.

I have to tell you this. Norbert Tucker died about a year ago, and Bebe Tucker has started doin' her grocery shoppin' at Bickel's grocery store.

Journaling

Sophi Link

Months after my birthday, the first page of my red-and-gold journal was still blank except for the printed word that trailed down the side of the paper: thoughts. I was seven years old, and I had no words to put in my pretty new book. Regardless, I kept it locked away although sometimes I would take it out just to leaf through the blank white sheets and wonder what to write first. By the time I finally put pencil to paper, my journal and I were already well-acquainted. My first few entries only spanned a few sentences, but they grew longer and more involved as time passed. Eventually, writing in my journal became a daily routine like eating lunch or brushing my teeth.

I've heard people say that introverts keep the best part of themselves for themselves; I kept the best part of myself for my journal. The words that I didn't voice to my friends and family during the day found their place on the page at night. After filling three pages with possibilities, I called her Camilla-May, the most beautiful name I could imagine back then. She was the only one who didn't talk to fill my quietness, so I finally had the time and the space to translate my thoughts into words. Somewhere between conception and expression, my ideas were getting lost inside me. Writing to Camilla was my way of pulling them back out and ensuring their place in the world. Keeping a journal reassured me that I was a real person with opinions and feelings even though they were buried. And the more I wrote, the more I understood about myself.

In the past eight years, I've filled seven books with musings. The eighth is still a work-in-progress, but the pages turn more slowly now. Instead of an outlet, I consider the journal a work of art. Each entry has a theme, some issue in my life that I need to reflect on, and I make myself take time to explore it fully. I like to think that in the future my journal will be an artifact of modern civilization, so I push myself to make it perfect. My primary concern is clarity. The spoken word is given meaning by the speaker's tone, pacing, and emotion. When I write, I strive to produce the same effect by choosing my words carefully and punctuating them precisely. My journal is the physical incarnation of my mind; the words written there will represent me when I can't represent myself. My thoughts make more sense when I write them down. And even though I appreciate having people whom I can talk to, some things will always stay between me and Camilla.

Facing Self-Doubt
Bobbie Troy

she leaped across
the bathroom rugs
like a frog on lily pads
to keep her feet
from getting cold

it was the hour
that everyone hates:
just before dawn
when yesterday's fears
have not been allayed
and today's not yet faced

she turned on the light,
looked in the mirror,
and saw it again:
the familiar sliver
of self-doubt

well, she thought,

at least it's a sliver

and not a slab

then she announced to the mirror:

i will let you stay for a while,

my old friend,

just to keep my ego in check

i will not, however,

let you keep me

from becoming a better writer

this year or any year

Originally published 1/24/2010 on www.voxpoetica.com

Composite Photograph: © Jeanne Tanks

One Day You Will Do This Too!
Ruby E. Pruitt

Liz's mother spoke with a smile, "One day you will do this too." Her mother's hands and apron were all covered with flour as she rolled out the crust for the next homemade chocolate pie.

Liz loved her mom's chocolate pies, all made from scratch with meringue on top.

Mother always made sure to leave enough for Liz to make her own personal-sized pie.

"Ah-h-h, the fond memories of Mother," thought Liz as she now stood looking at her own little girl.

Liz then left enough dough for a small personal-sized pie, handed the rolling pin to her daughter, smiled, and said, "One day you will do this too."

Beyond Reality

Magical stones and jars, spirits, goddesses, time travel, and strange creatures in elevators ... all things weird and wonderful can be found here.

Drawing: © Kathleen Willingham

The Guarding Stones

Caryn Moya Block

The swirling ghostly mist parted to reveal the circle of stones. They stood like silent sentinels on top of the hill. Each stone, appearing black and ominous, glistened with moisture. A sudden shift in the mist revealed the grass-lined path leading to the center. Evelyn stepped onto the path. As she passed the first circle of stones, she felt the air fill with energy. The hair on her arms stood up straight. This was a place of power.

The mist continued to swirl around the bases of the stones. Evelyn's feet, walking through eddies and swirls, would disappear only to appear again. The clunking of men in armor echoed around her. Fear gripped her heart. Looking around only showed her the blanket of mist, moving and writhing as if it were alive. She covered her mouth with her hand to stifle the scream that wanted to burst forth. Only by staying hidden would she be safe. She sent a silent prayer up to the Great Goddess. Surely, the heavy mist was a sign of favor, a promise of safety.

Gathering her courage, she quickened her pace on the path. The grass cushioned her steps along the way. She dared not run. She might be heard. Sound bounced from stone to mist and mist to valley below. She feared the sound of her breathing was enough to give her away. The stones would guard her. If she could just reach the altar stone at the center, she could call forth her magic. She would send the invaders back to the hell from which they sprang. She couldn't falter. This was her destiny. The village had sacrificed so many to give her this one chance. She wouldn't let them down.

She passed the second circle of stones. The air was so charged that sparks came off her skin. Her red hair rose and flew around her head. The mist stopped at the base of the second circle, writhing and pitching like a caged animal. The altar stone stood proudly in the center of the clearing, a shaft of sunlight surrounding it. Ancient carvings circled the base. Worn by wind and rain, they appeared to be mere shadows of what they once were.

Sobbing in relief, Evelyn flew the last few feet to her sanctuary. She hugged the base of the stone. Her tears formed rivulets of water cascading down the sides. Lifting her skirt, she crawled up to the platform and lay down, her head facing north. Her arms out at her sides reached for the east and west. Her feet, facing south, grounded her. She centered herself in her heart. Then, as peace infused her, she opened herself up to the power of the circle and began to sing. Her song gathered energy and flowed around the circle. Soon, the wind added its strength to the song, and a vortex of energy and air surrounded the altar stone.

Evelyn sang the second verse of the song, building the energy, calling the wind. Soon, the mist itself was added to the storm surrounding the altar. She sang the third verse, and the storm built again. Screams and shouts from the enemy were added to the storm. The winds raged, the mist swirled and the storm grew into a cyclone.

Evelyn sang the last stanza of her song and released the energy. The storm flew out from the altar stone like a bomb exploding. The invaders were flung from the mountain and landed in the valley below. Not a person was left standing, only the stones stood on guard. Evelyn, too weak to move, smiled up at the clear blue sky. It was done.

The East Side of Satisfaction

jd young

I always preen when people comment about my fingers. How they are long and beautifully shaped. How gentle yet striking their appearance. How gracefully they accept my rings. How expertly they calm when I stroke their hand. The simple touch of my fingers seems to quiet their soul.

I admit I find myself admiring my hands whenever I slip a Dunhill from its box and light my cigarette. Just holding the lighter delivers a beautiful, smooth, and satisfying feel. It was an unnecessary gift from an old flame, but most appreciated. Until the jewelers cleaned it, I had no idea it was solid gold, a lovely surprise when unsought gifts are tendered.

I got off the Metro at Dupont Circle, and my feet naturally turned east towards Becketts. It was dusk, and with autumn approaching, the air was cool. My decision to take a light jacket was spot on.

Sitting in Becketts was always satisfying. It was the last bookstore in DC where you could relax. I was free to read an obscure gothic novel, write notes, or simply mingle. Being able to order a glass of wine and enjoy a cigarette while I relaxed was an absolute luxury. The east side of this sanctuary opened onto 19th street and was dotted with small café tables. It allowed an unhindered view of both 19th and Q streets—likely the reason you could still smoke. And management had started offering simple food items to pair with a goblet of happiness.

No one bothered you to hurry along or empty your glass. It was casual, comfortable, and safe. Becketts had regulars, the insiders of the city. Each of us knew the others, and a simple tilt of the head or a knowing look was enough to acknowledge presence and acceptance.

Vacationers' money was neither needed nor encouraged. Grubby children fresh from the National Zoo, parents bitching and tired from schlepping through three of the Smithsonian buildings were not a welcome addition. Rarely did they stay for more than fifteen minutes, since the price of their drinks were double what regulars paid. Mel, our bartender, always watched out for the regulars.

We knew we needed some new blood in the enclave, but only a selected few became regulars. Not that we voted, but there were situations applicants had to face and manage. When all was done, and they surpassed expectations, they became one with us. They were welcomed and became part of our small and intimate group.

I disliked being tall during my school years. I felt awkward. Yet later I became most comfortable in this skin. My height, even while sitting, allowed me to gaze at the possibilities roaming about without straining myself. When I stood, my lanky and toned form gave off a confident air—which has served me well regardless of the company around me.

I instinctively chose a table on the east side where I could people-watch. Mel the bartender looked over, and I tilted my head. He knew exactly what I needed. Mel was a formidable-looking sort and appeared more suited to guarding a slaughterhouse in a mob neighborhood instead of catering to the eclectic needs of Becketts' customers.

Mel ran a tight ship. He knew all his customers' names, drinks, and just when to refill their glasses. He anticipated their moods and when they might require a bit more than alcohol to complete their evening. Mel took excellent care of Becketts' customers.

Money was never exchanged. Mel ran a tab, and you paid your debt when he determined it was due. But you always had to leave a substantial gratuity at the end of the evening. He was our protector. He let no one bother or upset his regulars. He took utmost care of everything, everyone, and every need at Becketts. And we were extremely grateful.

I sat quietly as Mel approached with a lovely Shiraz. I touched the cool vessel and let my fingers gently wrap around the bulb of the glass. Mel had filled it with an Australian blend that was one of my particular favorites. The dark-red liquid gently moved around the interior and promised a comforting evening, especially if I had several glasses. And, that night, I did.

My gaze was taken with a blonde crossing 19th street. She gently flipped her hair to the side, believing she was signaling confidence, yet it only magnified the resident fear in her soul. Her sadness was too apparent. She knew not where to go—but she did not want to go home to her empty apartment, the phone with no messages, the sounds of loneliness resident in each wall. She needed relief—anything that would make her happy.

I removed a Dunhill from the box and lifted it to my lips. As I raised my eyes, she appeared in the doorway. She too quickly took a seat at the bar and dropped her jacket and purse. She deliberately moved so her hair lay gently on her shoulders. She tried to appear as if this visit to Becketts was noted in her appointment book.

But I was adept at reading a soul's spirit—especially lost souls. This visit was a last-minute hope for her. She wanted compassion, a like spirit, anyone who might listen to her ever-increasing turmoil. She was physically beautiful yet bereft of love and emotion. Her only constant partner was the empty night, the dark that haunted her, stole her peace, devoured her soul.

I felt a bit selfish, but satisfied, because I knew I could calm her fears and satiate her soul. It was my choice to do so, or my choice to ignore her pain. It was my decision, and that was intoxicating for me. Mel looked toward me. I moved my jaw ever so slightly, and he immediately tended to her drink.

I was on my third glass of Shiraz when Mel nodded, indicating she was about to leave. I rose from my seat and slowly walked to her side. She looked at me and immediately started to apologize for blocking my way. I barely parted my lips to say "excuse me" when she started apologizing again.

I simply raised my fingers and lightly touched her chin.

I quietly offered, "No need to apologize. Please stay a moment and finish your wine. My name is Leslie. I haven't seen you before at Becketts."

She moved in her seat a bit awkwardly, then softly shared, "I, uh, um, this is my first visit. But, perhaps I should go. It is getting late."

I touched her shoulder and let my fingers slide toward the nape of her neck. She relaxed and lifted her glass to sip the last bit of wine. I looked toward Mel, and he instantly refilled her glass. She did not argue.

She attempted a smile and said her name was Lilly, and she had lived in the Dupont Circle area for several years. She had not been as involved in the city as she would like, but hoped to change that soon. Her shoulders dropped ever so slightly as fear and quietness again settled upon her.

Lilly accepted the offer to share my table. I set her glass on the small red napkin and offered her a cigarette. As I touched the Dunhills, she commented on my graceful fingers. I knew she would. I smiled, feigning ignorance of what she had observed, but I took great pride and satisfaction that she had noticed.

"Lilly, do you work in the city? Or perhaps you are independently wealthy and just like this area." She smiled ever so slightly, and a small sigh escaped her parted lips.

She looked at me and wondered if she dare trust me with so many secrets she kept so very close. I gently touched her wrist as she took a shallow breath and words started to flow. Each time she hesitated, I simply cupped her hand in mine and offered my complete attention.

Lilly had taken a position with the National Gallery. She was the senior fellow authenticating new acquisitions of Italian Renaissance sculptures. She loved her work.

She believed the sculptures were not just marble, but beautiful, living forces that were softly giving, truly knowing, and safe with which to share secrets. She could sit and speak, and they understood, they listened, they did not question, they did not judge.

Venetian sculptor Tullio Lombardo was one of her favorites. She was taken with his relief sculptures and would sit for long periods mentally chatting with them. Sometimes, she thought she would see a movement of an eye or lip, an ever-so-slight movement. She realized that sounded crazy, but in that split second she felt a deep connection, a sense of belonging, and no judgment. Just truth, which was simple and uncomplicated.

Though always forbidden to touch or hold without benefit of gloves, she loved to stroke the cool marble forms. The overwhelming urge to connect physically was unbearable. She was compelled to lay her hand upon the shoulder, stroke the arm or travel along the hip to touch the thigh of a magnificent piece. It spoke to her, it offered a sense of solace. It granted acceptance. It offered her more in its cold state than she had ever been able to achieve in her short life.

There was also physical gratification in these sculptures. They offered so much to the eyes and heart of the viewer. Watching them in quiet repose, you could feel their anguish, their laughter, their ultimate contentment. The warm-blooded that walk the earth were not remotely as generous.

The sculptor had captured the essence of his subjects' souls. This artisan was able to intimately understand and then totally share the emotions of his subjects. The attention to detail was nothing short of miraculous.

She said, "I feel so at home with them. They will be with me for hours and never demand anything from me. My emotions are left unscathed, my heart is not burdened and my mind remains clear. The only thing they leave with my soul is longing."

Lilly tilted her head slightly and continued to let her emotions flow. She was thankful for this tiny respite where she could emotionally hide. With her sculptures, there were no games. They allowed her to be one with them. The translucency of the stone was taunting.

Lilly continued, "With my forbidden naked hands, I delicately touch the drape of their tunics, slide my fingertips down their legs, or boldly lay my hand upon their faces. I encourage them to drink in the warmth from my being. The cold, smooth marble is invigorating. I am complete, I am satisfied."

Her current focus was the sculpture of St. Cecilia by Stefano Maderno. Standing before this powerful form was mesmerizing. Every soft fold of the marble burial gown, her peacefully positioned hands, and the portrayal of her head turned to the side, allowing one access to the fact she had been beheaded. It was brilliant to be cast in that moment, dead physically, yet alive in so many ways. The beauty of her sculpted form somehow denied her death.

Lilly stopped speaking and seemed physically spent. I looked up and Mel was in my gaze. Without words he delivered a sumptuous slice of dolce latté, rustic bread, seasoned oil, and fragrant olives along with refills of our wines. Lilly looked quite relieved. Her emotions were able to rest.

I prepared a small dish of food, and she gratefully accepted. Her outflow of emotions had ultimately overwhelmed all her senses. She was satisfied not to make any decisions, even that of choosing the food on her plate.

She sat very still. She appeared almost invisible and stared ahead with a soft yet vacant gaze in her eyes. Her hand slowly touched her napkin, but she seemed unable to lift her arm. She was as one with her sculptures.

I was preparing to suggest we walk the few steps to Dupont Circle and enjoy the end of our evening. The trees had started to change color, and there was always something, or someone, to watch. Street musicians, travelers from different walks of the city, or homeless sleeping on benches were the usual inhabitants.

The Circle had a long and spotted history. It had held Vietnam-era protests, gay and lesbian rallies, Sunday family gatherings around the fountain, fierce battles between street gangs and many homeless. The beautiful marble fountain was designed by the sculptor of the Lincoln Memorial. It was a fine place to spend a short bit of time, but never late in the evening. Then, the scene changed dramatically and you could not trust for your safety.

It was also a place where you could sit on a bench with a partner and remain isolated. The canopy of the tress covered a multitude of sins and rarely did people make eye contact. It was very private and yes, this would be a perfect spot to end my evening.

Mel looked over, and I immediately knew my tab was due. A gratuity would not be satisfactory this evening. It was time to pay my debt. His commanding stare confirmed there would be no discussion. My late night plans had taken a turn.

I rose from the table, took Lilly's hand and slowly escorted her to the sitting room by the bar, the entrance hidden from general view by the gorgeous baroque wood panels. It was a lovely and comfortable space, decorated with an elegant flare with sumptuous Persian carpets, a Victorian fainting couch, and exquisite artwork. The fainting couch was beautifully restored with silk fabric and highly-padded arms. There was a marble relief on the far wall, and Italian art by Donatello.

Lilly stood quietly and slowly turned her eyes around the room. She quietly asked if the reliefs were authentic. They looked like Tullio Lombardo's work, and she wondered how a bartender could afford originals by these masters. She slowly walked toward the artwork.

Mel entered, cupped Lilly's elbow and gently moved her toward the couch. She had not a chance to ask why, or even protest. She had had enough wine to allow her to feel quiet, and somewhat dreamy, and the physical results of her emotional release had drained all resistance from her body.

Mel sat next to her, raising his hand to her neck. He gently pushed her form so her head was resting comfortably on the silk-covered back of the couch, while her body gracefully arched. I felt complete jealousy invade my body, yet I knew my time would come.

She appeared to be at peace and comfortable. She gently murmured how she wanted her life to change. How happy she was that Becketts had been there for her that evening. How comfortable and inviting the patrons were. They instantly took her in as one of their own. She was drifting a bit and whispering about her sculptures when she cried out in pain.

Mel had fastened his mouth below her ear, on her jugular. He slowly stroked her arm, and then cradled her breast in his hand. She tried to pull away from the stabbing pain that she thought would kill her. And suddenly her screams transformed. They became ones of desire. The pain became enticing, pleasurable, and sexual. It was exquisite. It enveloped her and calmed her soul. This pain was more magnificent than her sculptures. And she wanted more.

She realized her lifeblood was quickly departing her body, yet her desire for this intense physical release was overwhelming. The more pain she allowed to ravage her soul, the more pleasure filled her mortal body. And she did not want it to end. Not ever.

Her screaming turned to small, soft utterances that filled the room. She became greedy for total fulfillment. Her skin slowly took on a translucency that was beautiful, desirable, and that tempted me to touch her arm, her thigh, her ankle. Her body went quite limp, and she took shallow breaths, but she knew this was not the end. She would be able to savor moments like this again. She would do anything to continue this complete state of being.

For a brief moment I thought Mel would offer me a last moment with Lilly, but I quickly realized that would not happen. He permitted debts to be paid in different ways. A feast such as Lilly was his preferred form of payment, but he was agreeable to other arrangements. When your debt was satisfied, he generally allowed the payment to simply expire. Others he allowed to go on until he tired of them. Lilly appeared to be something he wanted to keep for a time.

Disposing of paid debts was never an issue. Regular clients of Becketts had many different businesses, some in private industry, and many in the government. There were many debts owed him, and arrangements could always be made. Mel was a master handler.

Mel looked my way, indicating he was not yet finished. I quietly exited the room and rejoiced that the evening was again mine. My tab was clear, my hunger not yet quenched, but the night was still relatively young. There were still moments to relish and needs to be met. I again took my seat on the east side of the street and gingerly opened a new box of Dunhills.

As I turned, I noticed a somewhat brooding young man standing quite alone at the bar. I wondered if he might join me for a glass of contentment and an evening walk in Dupont Circle.

I somehow knew he would comment on my fingers.

...What Problem?
Marlee Laws

What do you do when strangers approach you?
Some would run away, worried
Others would ignore them
And some, well, me, would ask them what they want.
"YOU NEED TO COME WITH ME!"
"Why?"
"You wouldn't believe me if I told you." He grabs my hands
"If you want me to come you better start talking." I stand stock-still
"Well . . .your grandfather is going to commit a crime right now in his time, and if he does you won't be born, and if you aren't born then you will never have your children who will never betray the American government, thus the world war will never be started, and the world will never be destroyed!"
"So . . ."
"*I'm not done!* The new world will never be allowed to start and then I will die, so we have to go back in time and stop your grandfather, then I have to go forward to my time and you have to die in a world war that is due to start in the next 52.8 seconds! Otherwise the time streams will collapse and the universe will *explode*, thus sentencing all life to *extinction!*" He shrieks and tugs my hand.
I think about it
I wait, tapping my foot, and sure enough
The stranger disappears
Problem Solved

Drawing: © Jan Settle

A Gift for a Goddess: A Polynesian Snippet
Lisa Pugh

Prompt: "You don't convince people by what you say, but by what they understand"

Ali'i Kallaleya, chief of the Amooko Island People, awoke shivering. He knew he was not cold. The island never even grew chilly. The rain was always warm.

It was the dream. The call of a woman, an insistent demand, told him to come to her at the sacred mountain. As the tribe's leader, he must go, or all would be lost, his people destroyed. The village elder rose and dressed in his ceremonial best. He strode through the collection of quiet huts, making his way to the shaman's home.

Kotomahti was his uncle, his *kilo*—his seer—and the wisest man he had ever known when it came to the gods.

The *Mauna O Ahi*, Mountain of Fire, was the sacred home of *Akua Wahine* Pelemanua, Goddess of Volcanoes. Its peak rose over his village, a huge hulking monster that threatened the lives of his people every day of their lives. It had been restless for the past three moons, and the villagers had become more and more frightened.

The old soothsayer met his chieftain at the door. "She told me you'd come."

"Did she say what she required?"

"She said very little. She was very angry, though, so tread carefully."

Together, the two men climbed the path to the holy cavern. The gate was open. Looking at each other nervously, they walked inside.

The air within was oppressive and hot. Lava leaked into the chamber, partially encircling the stone altar that stood in the middle of the large cave. The table was covered in flowers and fruits, offerings to Pelemanua in hopes that she would calm herself and not create an eruption. On the far side of the room stood the goddess, the "earth-eating woman," glowering.

The strongly built female was bathed in flames. Her dark fiery eyes glared at them, and her long black hair floated around her. She was naked except for a skirt of fire. Lava glowed under her dark skin. Her broad nose was flared in annoyance.

"You took your time, ali'i Kallaleya," she growled.

"My apologies." The leader of his people dropped his head like a scolded boy. "I came as swiftly as I could."

"How can you say that? I have been sending you the call for five nights now."

"This was the first night I awoke and remembered your summons. The other dreams faded upon waking. I have no excuse besides that."

"Kilo," she turned to his companion. "Have you told him anything?"

"No, *Ka Mea Hanohano*, Most Excellent One. I felt such an order should be given by you directly."

"You did not want to be responsible," she remarked acidly. He shifted nervously. She merely nodded. "I think you are right. It is a serious thing I am demanding of him, and it is best that your ali'i, your chief, hears it from me. There must be no thought that you did this for your own gain."

"Thank you, oh great Pelemanua." The priest looked as if he had dodged a poison arrow.

The chieftain fought the urge to squirm. What could the goddess want? Her own holy man did not want to be the one to tell his leader what she would demand of him. It must be something pretty horrible.

Finally, her glowing eyes turned to him. "Ali'i Kallaleya, I need something from you."

"What is it, oh most lovely and gracious deity?"

"Your son, Duonuai." Seeing the shock on his face, she raised an eyebrow. "I feel I am being very generous. One young man for the lives of the entire village."

"You want me to sacrifice my son to you?"

"I want you to give him to me as a gift. He is not your oldest, though he is a great *koa*, a brave warrior, and a marvel to behold."

"But, all-powerful Pelemanua . . ."

"Enough! I have told you what you must do. I will expect you to deliver him in six days. If not, your people will not survive the seventh. The kilo and his highest acolytes will accompany you when you bring him here. Go!" She waved her hand. A strong hot wind picked up and blew both men out of the cavern. The heavy stone gates slammed shut behind them.

The chief landed heavily on the dirt path leading from the cave to the village. He lay there a long time, his head buried in his arms.

The shaman crawled carefully over to him. "My aliʻi, chief of my people?"

"Why did you not warn me, Kotomahti?" the leader cried, not looking up. "You are my uncle, and you let me walk in there blind!"

"I couldn't," the older man admitted. "Duonuai is my favorite of all your children. To know that he was to be killed . . . You would be given no alternative, so why extend your sorrow?"

"I see your meaning, but I don't like it."

"I know." The seer stood and offered a hand to his chief. Once both were on their feet, they headed back to the village.

"What am I to do?" Kallaleya asked, running both hands through his long hair.

"Do you have a choice?"

"My son or my people?" he sneered. "No. Besides, if I spared my son from her sacrifice, I'd lose him to her rage, along with everyone else."

"Very true."

"Duonuai shouldn't have to . . ." the chief growled, and then, catching himself, sighed frustrated. He could not speak against their goddess, no matter how much he hated her order.

After a pause, the shaman pointed out, "You will need to tell him. For a royal sacrifice at his age, he must agree."

"Will he?"

"Of all your children, he is the most pious, the most aware of his duty to his people. If you explain what is at stake, he will say yes."

"How do I tell my own son that he must die? How do I face him and explain why I'm permitting this?"

"Describe your dreams. Tell him what Pelemanua told you. Do not waste time on regrets and self-loathing for something out of your control." The old man smiled gently. "You are his father and leader of our people. When the time comes, you will know the words."

With a sad nod, the head of the tribe entered his home. His uncle remained outside for a moment.

"May the gods protect and guide you, my nephew," he muttered.

With a sigh, Kallaleya turned toward his own hut. He had to study the ritual of royal sacrifice so that each move and mood was perfect. Duonuai's death would be meaningless if Pelemanua was angry afterward.

As her husband entered, *Kuini* Abedalai, his queen and wife, looked up from the table. The males of the family had gathered to break their fast together. He alone had been missing. She and her daughters were serving food before moving to their own room to eat. "You were out early," she remarked mildly.

"I had a vision. I needed to consult with Kotomahti." He went to each member of the family and embraced them. Even his adult sons were not spared this unusual display of affection.

"Come and eat," she offered. "You look weary and need strength."

"Not quite yet, wife," he replied. "I must speak with Duonuai first."

"Me, father?" the young man replied, startled.

Kallaleya gazed at his son. Not yet twenty, he already had a warrior's body and a man's face. His hair was long and thick, black as cold lava rock. His eyes were bright, the brown of the richest soil. He still retained the vivacity of youth, but tempered it with circumspection and thought. It hurt Kallaleya just to look at him.

"Yes. Come, let us go in another room."

Enthusiastic and confused, Duonuai followed his father from the main room.

Several minutes later, the son stared at his father in shock. "She said what?"

"I was to give you to her within six days, or our people wouldn't survive the seventh."

"Why me? Did I offend her in some way?"

"I don't know," the chief replied miserably. "She did not seem angry with you. She was upset with me that I hadn't answered her summons for a few nights. Even that didn't seem the reason for her demand. She called you a gift."

"She demanded me as a gift?"

"Yes. Goddesses demand such things sometimes."

"I still don't understand."

"Neither do I. We've always shown her respect. We've kept her sacred days and performed the rituals with care." He shrugged helplessly. "Yet you don't question an Akua Wahine, a Goddess."

"Why tell me this? Why not order my obedience or lure me to her mountain?"

"You have seen seventeen summers. You have long been a man in this tribe. This ritual requires . . . victims . . . of your age to consent. I can't command you. I can't lead you to the ceremony unaware. You must agree, or all is lost."

Duonuai thought for a long moment. Emotions flashed in his eyes but never reached his face. In the end, he frowned. "Does it hurt?"

Chief Kallaleya closed his eyes briefly and sighed. "I know not. The customary sacrifice of a war prisoner, a *kauā* slave or a criminal, involves cutting out the heart, devouring a part of it, and throwing the rest into the lava. The sacrifice is then decapitated, and the blood pours into the magma as well. The body soon follows."

"Sounds painful," the young man remarked huskily with a slight tremor.

"I don't believe royal sacrifices are done so. It's been sixty harvests since the last time the goddess demanded one of royal blood. I've never seen it, but my father did. He never spoke of it. His brother was called, you see, an energetic youth with a tendency for mischief. From what little I have heard from the whispers of the elders, my summoned uncle lost his head to Pelemanua, but his heart was not removed."

"Why?"

"Perhaps because a leader must rely on his head more than his heart. Perhaps as a symbol of her supremacy over the head of our tribe. I'm not sure."

Duonuai nodded and muttered grimly, "I'm to be beheaded then."

"The kilo, our uncle, will try to find the fastest method allowed. He does not wish you to suffer." The older man paused, fighting for his voice. "And neither do I."

"A swift death for our people?" Inhaling a deep shuddering breath, the young man straightened. "I can do that."

Tears pricked the chief's eyes, but he refused to look away from the courage standing before him. "Thank you, son. The tribe will remember your sacrifice for all time."

"Father," the young man grasped his parent's forearms in the age-old warrior's embrace. "I do not hold you at fault. The goddess decreed, and she must be obeyed. I appreciate your honesty in admitting where your knowledge failed. I will go to the priest, and find out what I must do to prepare."

Kallaleya beamed with pride. "Go with honor, my son. Your mother may never forgive me, but it is good to know you will take no animosity toward me with you into the next life."

"Never, father. Not when a deity commands it."

For the next few days, preparations were made for the sacrifice. The shaman's and the chief's ceremonial garbs were repaired. The queen wept as she sewed additional decorations onto her husband's robe. Crying, her daughters worked on the cloak their brother would wear. Duonuai performed the ritual cleansing rites, ate the prescribed diet and bathed in the sacred springs. The path to the cave was strung with flowers and sacred plants. When all was ready, the tribal priest, his most experienced apprentices, the chief, and Duonuai proceeded up the path to Pelemanua's cave. The whole village lined the route to watch the death march, the sacrifice that would save everyone's life.

The young man walked in the center of the group, his body erect, his face set like granite. He was dressed in the finest cloak. His hair fell long and loose, flowing in the breeze. Feathers adorned his clothing and hair. A stone-and-rope crown circled his brow. He could have been going to his wedding rather than his execution.

The members of the party bowed before stepping through the doorway. Torches lined the bridge over the molten rock. The altar lay before them, candles and pots of pungent oils lining its edges and that of the island on which it stood.

At the sight of the sacrificial table, Duonuai faltered for the first and only time. A single tremor ran through him, his gaze riveted on the heavy black stone. He inhaled deeply and stepped across the narrow rock bridge.

Chief Kallaleya closed his eyes briefly. Would he have had the courage to approach his death with such calm? He did not know, but he was determined to stand by his son's side and watch the young man's greatness shine.

Walking slowly to the center of the temple, the young man stared down at the altar. "May I touch it?" he asked the kilo.

"Yes" was the hoarse response. His great-uncle was having a difficult time keeping his composure as well.

Duonuai caressed the tabletop. Along with the natural pitting and air holes that had formed in the lava rock, several long scrapes and small slits marred the surface. He shivered when he considered what had made those marks.

"Duonuai?" his father began.

"Let's just finish this," the lad replied quietly.

Chief Kallaleya made a move to comfort his son. Kilo Kotomahti laid a hand on the shoulder of the ali'i, and, with an emotion-laden look, shook his head. The tribal leader nodded. No need to embarrass his son with a show of regret and grief.

Kotomahti walked around until he faced his great-nephew. "Pelemanua has called you here," he intoned.

"I hear and obey," Duonuai replied, his face a mask.

"Pelemanua demands your mind."

"I give it gladly, no thoughts but hers."

"Pelemanua demands your body."

"I give it gladly, hers to command."

"Pelemanua demands your heart."

"I give it gladly, beating only for her."

"Pelemanua demands your life."

The slightest hesitation. "I give it gladly, my existence for the protection of all."

"Pelemanua demands your soul."

"I give it gladly, my essence is hers to do with as she will."

"Pelemanua accepts all you offer."

The litany over, the tribal holy man sprinkled fresh clean water on the prince, using a palm branch. He put the sacred berries in the boy's mouth. Then, guiding the sacrifice to his knees, he stepped behind him. An acolyte gave the shaman a long, curved obsidian sword. With trembling hands, the old man raised the blade to strike.

Suddenly, a blast of hot air swirled through the chamber. The whirlwind blinded everyone. Flames leapt. Smoke billowed up from the candles and pots.

Out of the molten rock rose a fierce beautiful woman. Ten feet tall, she was dressed in a fire-colored sarong. Her black hair floated around her. Her eyes glowed like hot copper. Her honey skin shone.

"Stop!" she declared.

Kotomahti froze, staring at the approaching goddess. "Ka Mea Hanohano—Most Excellent One?"

"What are you doing?"

"You demanded this young man as a sacrifice."

"I insisted you give him to me as a gift. I don't remember telling you to kill him."

"Oh." The seer lowered his weapon, with a trembling sigh of relief.

Chief Kallaleya bowed to her. "Oh great Pelemanua, we obviously misunderstood. We apologize."

"And well you should! You almost needlessly killed your own son, Kallaleya," she snapped, glaring at the priests and leader of the tribe. "Now, all of you, go! Leave me with my gift."

With muttered salutes, the dismissed men quickly made their exit.

When they reached the outside, the small group inhaled cool air gratefully. Then, they began down the steep path.

"That was nearly a disaster," Kotomahti remarked to his kin.

"Yes," the ali'i agreed. "It was foolish of us to assume what she wanted."

"At least Duonuai is safe."

"For how long? Pelemanua isn't known for her patience and tolerance of mortals."

"That depends on your son's adaptability and ingenuity."

"What does she want him for?" Kallaleya asked, removing his headdress and brushing a frustrated hand through his hair.

The shaman chuckled. "I think we've been very blind indeed. I was so sure she wanted Duonuai in the same way she wanted my brother, that I didn't consider another occurrence of royal summoning. Then again, it hasn't happened in five hundred winters."

"What do you mean?"

"Have you heard the story of Pelemanua and Halkunaleya?"

Chief Kallaleya frowned, trying to remember that particular tale. When he recalled it, his eyes widened, and a broad grin spread over his face. "You think she wants my son for *that*?"

"It makes sense. The prince is wise, strong, and clever. He is a great koa, a great warrior. Perhaps more importantly, he is a young, handsome, virile male."

"Let's just hope he has extraordinary stamina as well," the chief laughed, relieved, and amazed at the strangeness of fate.

The party moved back to the village, feeling far less gloomy than when they left it.

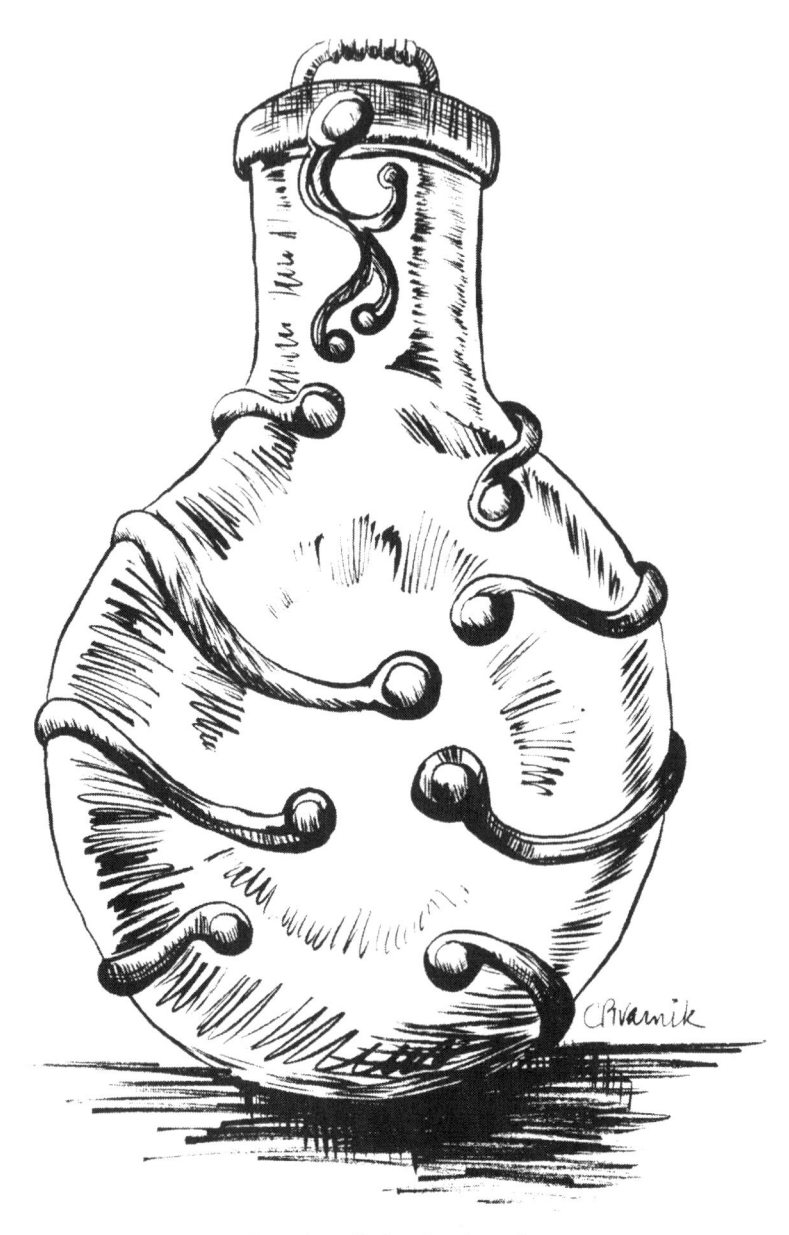

Drawing: © Carole Pivarnik

The Gift

Jack Daily

Lydia pulled into the driveway of the renowned brick home her husband Paul, the architect, had built just a year ago. It was located on a secluded cul-de-sac in a neighborhood often featured in Sunday's section of "Homes and Gardens." She had just finished running errands after lunch with Margaret. On the seat beside her rested a blue bottle, the kind you search for in antique and curio shops. Streaked with fine layers of dust, it had a translucent finish, and was capped with a gray, iron-like lid that would take effort to pry open.

Lydia sat, not ready to get out of the car, replaying the after-lunch conversation.

Margaret had pulled a blue bottle from an oversized handbag and thrust it across the table. "This is a gift for you, a very special gift. Lydia, do you believe in ghosts?"

Lydia had been surprised at the question and wasn't sure what to say, "I'm not sure. I've never seen one, but I like to keep an open mind."

She knew it sounded safe, but what is one to say to such a question, particularly from someone you don't know that well? Today was well beyond a get-acquainted lunch. Though she had known Margaret for over six months, they were not exactly close friends. The truth was, Lydia didn't believe in ghosts.

Margaret had smiled back at her and in an offhand way said, "Lydia, inside this blue bottle lives a ghost. It's a good ghost, so don't be afraid. You are one of us now; it is time to receive your ghost. Do you understand me?"

Now this was just getting too weird, thought Lydia.

"Well, I can tell you it's a beautiful bottle. Paul will know just where to showcase it in our home. Margaret, I'm going to get the check. It was a lovely lunch, but I need to get going. Paul is coming home early after a busy week with clients. I promised him a romantic dinner."

"Okay Lydia, but just one more thing. The ghost works good magic, but only from inside the bottle. If you were to open the bottle, the ghost is required to leave, find a new place. It would be upset and terrible things could happen. At least, that's what I was told when I received my bottle. Enjoy!"

Lydia finally opened the car door, entered the house through the side door off the patio, and walked into the kitchen where she set the canvas bag, with the groceries and the blue bottle, on top the kitchen counter. Her thoughts quickly turned to the dinner she was about to prepare: grilled lamb chops, basmati rice in a wild mushroom sauce, and sautéed spinach. It was one of Paul's favorites.

Lydia proceeded to the bedroom to change clothes. She wanted to wear something eye-catching tonight, even though she would be in the kitchen for a good hour. A quick nap would be refreshing, she thought, as she plopped down into the overstuffed chair they both used while changing clothes.

A banging noise startled Lydia. She glanced at her watch to find she had dozed off for almost an hour. She jumped up and headed toward the kitchen.

"Paul, it's you! You did make it home early. I'm so excited. We are going to have one of your favorite meals."

"Hi, sweetheart," replied Paul. "I'm chilling a bottle of Pinot Gris. By the way where did you get that wonderful blue bottle? I think that's Depression-era glass. Was it very expensive?"

"No, no, it was a gift, a gift from Margaret. You won't believe the story she told me about the bottle. I'll save it for dinner."

"Sounds like fun," replied Paul. "I gave it a damp-cloth cleaning before arranging it on the middle shelf of the étagère. That shelf gets the best light, and the cobalt-blue reflections are remarkable. See what you think."

Lydia's eyes focused on the middle shelf. "Paul ... where's the iron-looking lid that sealed the bottle?"

Weird

jd young

What does she mean, I'm weird? I'd been called pushy and aggressive, even bitchy, but never weird. Kym looked at me, sorry she had let the words leave her mouth. She shook her head, and we both stood quietly, staring at the blinking floor lights on the elevator display.

We had entered the elevator on the 32nd floor after another grueling workday. I was frustrated and angry about the work and was glad to be done. Nothing I could possibly do had made anyone happy. Not the remotest hint of a smile or nod of gratitude was ever offered.

When I shut the office door, I looked forward to another uneventful weekend. Though I had enough work stuffed into my briefcase for a week, I could do it in my T-shirt and jeans, savoring a cup of coffee with the fluid sounds of Boccelli filling my otherwise empty living room. A last-minute invitation for drinks this evening slightly buoyed my mood.

I had chosen consulting as my career, thinking I would be able to help people. However, it seemed those that benefited the most from my expertise were the highest-paid CEOs on the planet. My career had become just a job and was the latest in a long succession of wrong choices. The all-too-familiar badge of failure appeared on my chest.

Kym and I stood, eyes closed, backs pressed against the redwood-paneled walls and elbows resting on the polished-brass rails. Our shoulders were slumped, and our overstuffed briefcases were lying at our feet. As I slowly opened my eyes, I noticed the round piece of black glass located above the fire-alarm bell. It was a staple in most elevators. Kym opened her eyes and vacantly offered up that the glass might be a hidden security camera.

As I focused my full attention on the smoky, dark glass, I noticed the many scratches that covered the innocuous dark space. The scratches appeared to be on the inside of the pane. I asked Kym if she thought those scratches might be the result of something or someone behind the glass. Could it be an entity trapped and trying to gain attention, or perhaps clearing the glass of fog while peering at the captive occupants in the elevator?

Her eyes widened, and she blurted out that I was just really weird. I expected that from others, but not her. I returned her stare, then turned my attention to the dark glass.

The floor numbers blinked by: 12, 11, 10, and then we stopped. It was not jolting or frightening, just a quiet stop. The doors did not open, the elevator did not venture downward, and no alarm sounded. I was particularly annoyed. I was looking forward to meeting a couple of friends and enjoying dinner and a bottle of wine. Obviously, I would be late, again.

We stood motionless for a few moments, then fruitlessly pushed several buttons, hoping the machinery would respond. The elevator made no movement, and the bell was silent. The emergency phone was futile. Though it rang, there was no answer.

Kym and I stared at each other in total frustration. It was after seven, and we knew the maintenance crew had left. Normal people led normal lives and worked normal hours. We, on the other hand, were always at work. We had to believe we were critical personnel. If we left after only twelve hours, some CEO might have to wait an additional two minutes for his outrageous compensation package.

It was late Friday, and I wondered if anyone would look for us. I had not had a significant other in a long time. My dwindling circle of friends were used to my being late or simply not showing up. Kym had just left a relationship and was on her way to rent a video, and then to the ABC store to greet Johnny Walker.

We resigned ourselves to another solitary Friday night. We would again sit on a carpeted floor, pen in hand, shoes kicked off, reviewing stock statements for a fat cat. The geography was just different.

We hadn't spoken for several minutes when I heard an irritating noise. I turned and glared at Kym, but she had dozed off. The precious stock statements had fallen to her thigh, and her ballpoint was leaking on the carpet.

Maybe someone had noticed we were trapped and was trying to start the elevator. My eyes were tired, and I tilted my head back to rest. I was bothered that Kym was asleep. Even on the best of days, sleep was not easy for me, and I wonder if . . . What is that irritating noise? It had started again.

Kym was breathing rhythmically and not moving a muscle. My eyes turned toward the black glass above the alarm button. There appeared to be a new scratch, a deeper one, across the center of the glass. I rubbed my eyes, trying to clear my gaze, when there appeared to be a flash from the glass. Not like that of a camera, but like an animal's eyes when caught in headlights.

There was something in there. It was not yet clear, but definitely something. Was something trapped in there? Had no one ever paid attention? Had no one tried to help? How could one ride the elevator each day and not notice? I knew I had to help this poor soul, but I could not move. I ignored the fear that now pulled at my throat.

What if this entity was there for a reason? Had someone forcefully restrained it? What had it done? What if it wanted to hurt me? Why did Kym not wake up? Why could I not keep my thoughts straight? My center of attention became the four-inch piece of glass.

My mind tried to make sense of my surroundings. Even if something was behind the glass, surely it could not climb through it. The space could only be a few inches wide. Nothing could possibly survive in there. What would it eat?

I again concentrated on the smoky glass, and the shapes became clearer. They were eyes. Dark eyes. Sad eyes. Haunting eyes. They were needful but somehow extraordinarily confident. And the eyes were fixated on me. Without an audible word, we communicated. I don't remember moving, but I was suddenly in front of the button panel below the dark glass. The hours of stillness had caused the air to become stagnant, and my face was hot and wet. I leaned my cheek against the cool metal panel. It was deliciously comforting, and an almost immediate sense of peace took my breath away.

The last time I had felt this way was . . well, I didn't know if I had ever felt this peace. It was absolute serenity. Gentleness. Tranquility. A peculiar sense of belonging I'd never known before, and an odd and extraordinary sense of extreme hunger. I wanted more, much more. I wanted all of it. I wanted to become part of it. I tried to will myself into it. I focused all my concentration to that end.

I was amazed at the ease with which the transformation happened. I don't remember any pain, and the small trickle of red down the cool metal panel was hardly noticeable.

It was two hours later when the elevator finally moved. Kym felt the jerky motion and quickly awakened. She felt something moist under her leg and shook her head to clear the sleep. When she finally focused on the gruesome sight beside her, she opened her mouth to scream but made no sound.

The lifeless form next to her was propped against the paneled wall. The right hand clutched those important stock statements; two fingers on the left hand were gone. Matted hair covered two empty spheres above the nose, and the encroaching liquid was turning Kym's skirt red. When the doors finally opened, Kym crawled out. Maintenance workers crowded the small space. They stared at the mess on their newly installed carpet, and the deep scratches on their polished brass rail.

I felt badly for Kym, but I was quite peaceful in my new surroundings. Though at first reluctant to give up my flesh to this spirit, I had finally understood what was required of me. I had to give only flesh and bone. In return I was fulfilled. My hunger was satisfied. I had peace, tranquility and comfort. No more lonely weekends, sixty-hour workweeks, or a dwindling circle of friends.

I would now look forward to seeing people each day, and feel their gratitude when the elevator doors opened on time, and they arrived in the lobby without injury. I would be privy to their quiet thoughts, their hopes and their fears. When it was time, I would make my scratch in the glass. One passenger would notice, and I would help in her transformation.

In Another Light
Jack Daily

The window shade filtered the neon street lamps that filled the room with an eerie glow. I was overcome by regrets of familiarity: the small bed with a single pillow atop the neatly creased, flannel blanket I had slept under as a child; centered on the opposite wall, the dime-store picture of Jesus that Mother had given me after the church service that buried my father; and the hand-me-down oak chest that had stored the toys and books I went to for comfort.

"Jack, you were only eight years old—a child in third grade, overwhelmed by spelling tests and those stupid fractions in flash-card math."

Elizabeth grabbed my hand and with a quiet look continued, "You can't undo the past; you must finally let it go."

The creep of inhuman existence once again began its slow crawl at the base of my neck as I smiled at her, eyes burning blood crimson.

With the sudden clarity of a full moon on a cloudless night, Elizabeth tilted her neck in submission and whispered, "I'm ready Jack."

Seeing Reality
Marlee Laws

A city of wax
Placed by the hand of a child
Thrives during winter

With its chessboard citizens
And dollhouse furniture
Filled with the fantasies of the young

Towers and cottages
The good emerging triumphant
For an eternal instant legends are real

Then comes summer
Thawing reality and chaos with it

The wax city is destroyed

Decimated
Razed to the ground

An Invitation to Ponder

Authors never know when the muse will tap on their shoulder and point them to inspiration. The following pieces result from such encounters.

Painting: © Kathleen Willingham

In the Forest
Judith Dreyer

Lovely water falls
As graceful lilies
Pad the pond.

Bullfrogs hide
As tree stumps grab
The stream's contentment.

Shifts ease the moment. I am grateful.
Touching/holding/laughing with the breeze
Of summer's shifting hold of season.

Tall pines form an arbor here
Graceful limbs an embrace
Of cool shadows and filtered light
when forest turns into night.

Circles and Hands
Bobbie Troy

if you hold your hands
behind your back
and walk in a circle three times
it will help you remember
what has eluded you
or so they say

if you hold your hands
in front of you
and walk in a circle three times
it will help you forget
your sorrows and woes
or so they say

if it were that simple
I would be circling every day
to remember the good things
and forget the bad

but the hands become old
and the circles get broken
and time passes on
or so they say

My Mind Is Free
Bobbie Troy

unlike my body

that is tethered to the ground

by gravity

my mind is free

unlike my heart

that is wrapped

around yours

my mind is free

unlike the minions

of guilt and remorse

on my doorstep

my mind is free

but where is the freedom

that I am supposed to feel?

Originally published 2/13/12 on http://cavalcadeofstars.wordpress.com/

Musical Memories
a sestina

Sophi Link

Editor's Note: The sestina is a complex form that achieves its often spectacular effects through intricate repetition. The sestina follows a strict pattern of the repetition of the initial six end-words of the first stanza through the remaining five six-line stanzas, culminating in a three envoi. The lines may be of any length, though in its initial incarnation, the sestina followed a syllabic restriction.

Stars share their light with the night
Shining in the darkness far above
Every object stretches its long shadow
I let my thoughts fly up and away
They wind a path past the crescent moon
Dancing in time to the celestial music

I'm serenaded by the cricket's music
They trace a rhythm in the blooming night
And remotely untouchable lies the moon
Gleaming white in its world far above
Whether or not we choose to melt away
Into the faintest of shape-shifting shadows.

But now something solid forms from shadow
And everyone appears with laughs like music
Worries laid aside until they rot away
And vanish into the fabric of a summer night.
Smoke begins to twine through the stars above
From the fire that burns brighter than the moon

We smile at each other like sideways moons
Banishing the dark from our mind's shadows
And flooding them with the radiance from above
As we join together to revel in the music
Woven from the threads of this long-awaited night
Before it too-soon begins to fall away

Our voices are a brew to keep the blues away
And the main ingredient? Light from the moon
To keep us here through the hours of the night.
All through long winter, these times were shadows
To be chased tirelessly, though they ran away
And our hopes dangled just a little too far above.

And now the clouds are tinged with pink above
the mountain's horizon such a long way away.
The morning announces itself with trumpet music
That drives away the pale form of the moon.
In creep the worries that sneak around shadows,
their grasp tightens in the absence of night.

In the sky above, morning triumphs over night.
Receding from sight, far away flee the shadows
Imprinted with musical memories of the moon.

It Exists

Pennie Patterson

Look to the moon in awe
Observe the splendor of the stars
And feel the power that lurks there.

Spy upon the ants
The inner sap of the trees
And find the wonder that works there.

Look to the human heart
Beneath the greed, the outer shell
Know the tenderness that purrs there.

Is it God or is it chance?
Does it matter?
For it stirs there.

The Future Storm
Pennie Patterson

Blue the sky
With silent clouds rushing by.
Green are the trees and still
The bush, the field, the air
All of nature lies silent
Awaiting the future storm.

Come a man.
A small and lonely figure
Insignificant against the sweep of the sky.
His steps stir the earth.
His hand rends the bush
And then he passes on.

A small and lonely figure
Insignificant against the sweep of the sky
Changed now to the colors of the night
Which swallow the man in silence
And all of nature is still
Awaiting the future storm.

Drawing: © Arlene Baker

Absinthe

D.C. Ackerly

Part of me is like absinthe, a murky, forbidden elixir.

I am absinthe, poured into a jam jar, sealed with a doily
and stored next to the paisley settee.

I am not who my husband needs me to be—peaceful.

I am not who my mother wants me to be—steadfast.

I just sit in my jar, waiting for someone to knock it over,
and let it shatter on the hardwood floor.

Then I can ooze through the cracks and escape to the cellar
where murkiness thrives.

A Thirty-Percent Chance of Rain

Jack Daily

Most people watch the local news as a nightly ritual. The attractive newscasters begin with stories from around the globe, then give national perspectives, and finally the local area weather. We are particularly focused on that last segment. The variables of rain, snow, sunshine, winds, and severity are expertly shaped and shown to us by hands waving in cold fronts, proclamations of sunny skies, and the percent chance of rain. And that's the question we really want answered with some certainty. "Will it rain tomorrow?"

Don't expect a definite answer because the chance of rain is fed to the weather channels from Las Vegas bookmakers whose livelihoods depend on probability and percentages. Over time, I've concluded that thirty percent or more means it's going to rain. Our desire for this knowledge is rooted in pragmatic consequences. What we learn before we push the remote's off button sets our mind in motion as to what we will wear the next day. For example, do I need a hat, how many layers of which garments, and will rush-hour traffic be snarly?

Before TV and radio, I imagine, one would just open the door the next morning and take a look. The night-before, tossing and turning anxiety was held in reserve for the wired generations of today.

Progress does not advance without a downside.

Too Many Secrets

jd young

It is the unexpected tragedy or too-seldom fleeting happy moment that keeps us connected on the most frail of tightropes. The untimely death of a sibling causes a confrontation of past and present. The roles we developed to keep us sane as adults, and the past roles of children in which we struggled to survive, are pitted amidst battling and intense emotions. There is never a good outcome, no matter how hard we hope and try. The injured psyche has a long memory and does not heal without total participation.

We settle into a protective sphere of comfort. We surround ourselves with things and people we need so as not to let the cold, scary past touch us lest those memories resurface. We cannot leave this artificial comfort zone because we will fall and never recover. That fear consumes our being.

Life continues under our covenants, but the old pains linger. We are forced to gather at a difficult time. Some of us hope to "re-bond" and "re-care" for each other—but finally accept there is no hope. It will not happen. It cannot happen. The gut-wrenching ache, disappointment, and nausea would be lethal. We would not survive, and we each recognize that.

At a funeral, we sit with each other, cry at the appropriate times, and pray we may have found common ground, but it flashes past quickly. We are glad when we must catch our planes and leave the group. The last few minutes with each other are physically painful. We cannot "ask the question," or inquire why something was said. We must hug, kiss, and say goodbye as though nothing has happened except the sadness of the sibling loss.

Everything else remains unsaid, and silently all agree. All are fearful of that one comment that might slip, that one sentence that would set off the rage of years. The group would erupt with accusations, unforgiveness, and fear.

Our childhood—the dark, low whispers and lingering, intense fear—sits heavily upon our shoulders and commands our attention. Our defenses ember, ready us for combat, and push out any emotion that does not support our victory in this imminent battle.

Love becomes weakness. Physical touch becomes adversity. Silence is the only refuge.

Break Your Silent Thoughts
Jack Daily

Translucent daggers hang from roof-top's edge
Unafraid to jump, to take the frozen plunge,
Their sharp sounds will break your silent thoughts
Else the sun steals the moment, weakens the blow.

Originally published on vox poetica.

A Change in Weather
Jack Daily

The Gulf Coast sails boats on blue water,
sprinkles white sand on beaches,
eats rib-sticking barbecue,
warms its shore with a southerly breeze,
listens to late-night blues.

But on a rare February day,
it can conjure a bitterly cold wind,
skim it across once-friendly waters,
smack you in the face with an icy hand
while leaves of magnolia shade begin to cry.

Drawing: © Dina Buckley

Angel of . . . What?
Martha Orr Conn

I once knew a doctor who had a nurse
Who seemed to care if you felt worse!
When you called her on the phone,
She'd listen to your plaintive moan
And, in a voice concerned, she'd say,
"My dear, you come right in today."

Where , oh where has that angel flown?
Now when Nurse answers the telephone,
It's, "Doctor can see you a month from now,
If you're sure it's really worth his while."
Or a brisk, "That sounds like nothing but flu;
Just let me tell you what to do."
Or, "Hold on, please." And the line goes dead
While you know she's saying, "It's all in her head!"

Oh, what I'd give to answer the phone
When Nurse calls her doctor and starts to moan.

Unfinished Statements

Marlee Laws

Things never work when . . .

In a perfect world I would be . . .

All I see in my head is . . .

Let it go.

You should know that . . .

Everything I ever forgot to say is . . .

My last request is . . .

I can accept that . . .

What I meant to say was . . .

If I asked you . . .

Would you?

Dressed for Work

Bobbie Troy

It was the first day of spring so she decided to wear her new pink-linen suit. It made her skin more radiant than usual and put a little extra bounce in her step. She wore pale-gray pumps, with a matching bag, of course. The gray accessories accented her ash-blond hair. Her makeup was so light she appeared to wear none. The picture was perfect: an attractive woman beautifully turned out.

She sat behind a huge, modern desk in an office on the 20th floor of a high-rise office building. Her name plate read: Ms. Susan Reed, Senior Vice President.

The sun shone in from the windows, the light bouncing off her desk and into her blue eyes. A perfect movie set.

As I walked into the room for our meeting, she looked up at me and smiled. But the sparkle in her pale-blue eyes suddenly diminished, and for a brief moment, failed to hide the loneliness behind them.

Drawing: © Carole Pivarnik

Snow

Caryn Moya Block

The snowflakes laugh
As they dance and twirl
Floating and flurrying
As they gather together.

For this last chance to be solid
And fall in perfect form
To lay a blanket on Earth
And keep her tootsies warm.

For Spring has stretched and raised her head.
The buds are on the trees and the
Daffodils smile their cheery hello.
While the robin dances the tango.

A cosmic prank to show
The cold wind doing his share
To let the snowflakes dance and swirl
As they tumble and chuckle.

Star Power

Gwen Monohan

A comet's streaking tail,
brushing the sky at night,
brought our lives in focus
like a camera.

We gathered on high ridges
near back-country roads
looking for direction
in the darkened view.

Holding binoculars
and even telescopes,
we searched our lighted past
with childlike wonder.

Seeking understanding
of some higher power,
Or at least ancient vision
from the star dust.

Direction is Everything
Jack Daily

If my head faces East

I see hope, new beginnings

I get my tools and thump my chest

If my head faces West

I see an unfinished day in ruins

I go fetal and close my eyes

If my head faces North

I see promise

I must weigh action

against consequence

If my head faces South

I feel awash in warm saltwater

And this day will last forever

Originally published on vox poetica.

Looking Within

MaryAnn Morrison

What happens to a person on the edge?
I'm not exactly sure what the edge looks like
But I'm very certain I'm there.
I know this because I'm never on solid ground anymore.
I'm always in a place of flux,
Indecision, and frustration.
Tears rest in wait to spill forth
Temporarily cleansing the mud and muck
That fill my brain with confusion.

I am the true Piscean
Being pulled by equal strengths in opposite directions,
Ripping apart the wholeness of my being.

Sometimes they rest
Those forces of indecision.
Sometimes they are so strong
They leave me powerless
And I feel drawn to that space,
Watching someone else's genius
In a prone position for the day.

The forces rest,
Only to regenerate
With even greater power.

In Quiet Shadows
Jack Daily

In quiet shadows
of morning light,

mistakes rearrange,
fight for importance
then fall to the bottom.

Easy acts of kindness,

"What can I do?"
"That's a good idea."
"You shined today."

become the sharper focus
gain in importance
rise to the top.

We will do it again today.

And I eagerly await,
The quiet shadows and
magic of morning light.

Originally published on vox poetica.

A Song in Celebration of Soaring
Pennie L. Kinsey

I have soared above the Earth
to reach the Infinite
and, ecstatic, have found the heights.
As I soared, I beheld
the Essence of the Almighty.
Opening my eyes, I saw great Light:
the sun shone forth an array of colors
unequaled by any artist.

In the distance, I felt the heavens emerge
from snow-capped mountains, as the wind
blew past
the softness of the clouds
And of the firmament.
It was as if the Universe
put on her "Sunday best"
bursting with splendor.

To love All that exists
one must only be
able to reach out in faith
celebrating Creation;
rejoicing with the angels

Let your spirit be limitless,
go beyond your imagination,
go beyond your self, strive for justice.
Defy the known, the concrete,
Defy matter.

Then extend from your self
the vision of Truth, of Giftedness,
from the One
Who calls you beyond . . .

Now,
trust enough to let
loose, have faith enough to trust,
belief enough to have faith;
enough to think, to do;
do enough to attain,
attain enough to grasp
the immensity of
hope . . .

Live exuberantly.
Glorify,
Celebrate,
Soar!

Photograph: © Diane Burdette

Softball Slugger
Diane Burdette

Brand new uniform
purple and gray
Softball novice
eager to play.

New to sports
awkward and shy
Can't hit the ball
or catch a fly.

Plenty of advice
flows her way
Everyone has
a lot to say.

Pay attention
stand up straight
Make the pitcher
have to wait.

Watch the ball
hold the bat
Be ready to swing,
but not at that.

When you walk
touch the base
Hopefully
a run takes place.

From first to second
over to third
Be excited
for what occurred.

Teammates ready
hear them shout
Run for home
don't get out!

If needed
you can slide
Watch the catcher
don't collide.

Have fun
be glad we came
After all
it's just a game.

Our girl is next
the field creeps in
She strikes once
then again.

The pitcher throws
the pitch is good
The bat connects
just like it should.

A homerun
listen to the crowd
Teammates are happy
parents are proud.

You're a slugger
there is no doubt
What's your secret
Tune everyone out!

Random Thoughts on Life

(or What We Should Teach Our Children)

Bobbie Troy

Never stop learning.

Hearts break easily but mend with difficulty.

Everyone should have a "bucket list."

Don't blame your problems on others.

Art is everywhere, not just in museums.

Think before you act.

Stress can kill.

Life is short. Have fun.

Listen to others, but make your own decisions.

Be curious. Ask questions.

Throw this list away, and make your own.

Better yet, don't make a list at all.

Originally published 2/13/12 on http://cavalcadeofstars.wordpress.com/.

The Sands of Time

Childhood confidence tempered by experience brings varied perspectives. These pieces take us through the sands of time.

Drawing: © Kathy Webber

In Childhood

Diane Burdette

Eyes full of wonder
like prisms they shine

Life of fables,
stories, and rhyme.

Time to be carefree
tumble and play

Imagination soars
each minute, each day.

Eyes full of wonder
like fireflies at night

Childhood is special
and what a delight!

Growing Up

MaryAnn Morrison

Remembering the good things, the people in my life,
I always think of Mum, dedicated wife.
I remember her wisdom, always ready to share
with her children around her who thrived in her care.
I think of my father, like never before.
A very kind man who would open the door
to anyone passing, or any in need.
He showed us kindness by planting the seeds.
Those seeds became scattered, all hither and yon,
in life's valleys and hills, until new life was born.
As the cycle of parenting brings forth new lives,
Grandparents hope all their seeds will survive.
Children can thrive on the love they are given.
They learn by example, the choices for living.
Life should be filled with what everyone needs
The love of oneself, the real nurturing seed.

Confidence

Bobbie Troy

confidence

belongs to the very young

until, that is, they bathe

in the waters

of life's disappointments

then confidence moves

behind the curtains

sometimes twitching a bit

wanting to resurface

but waiting to be called upon

always waiting and ready

Originally published 2/13/12 on http://cavalcadeofstars.wordpress.com/.

Photograph: © Jack Daily

Before I Could Fly

Judith Dreyer

Grandpa,
Tall and lean
You held me high
I reached for the skies
And worlds within
Beyond my grasp
Or so I thought in my growing-up time
when you held my hand.

Grandma,
Pots you filled
Bright and fresh
You smelled of meadows
And rain,
Flower scents linger in my heart
As I see daffodil lights
Behind my eyes
And the bouquets we made as
Your hand guided mine.

Now I understand.
My heart smiles as memories
Brush my mind when you held
My hands before I could fly.

vox poetica submitted July 22, 2011 with Jack Daily's picture of ladder and pot on porch.

A Change of Heart

Nancy Scott

It was late summer, just before my first year in grade school. Mother and Grandma were driving into the country to buy tomatoes for canning. I was in the street, playing kick-the-can with some neighborhood kids when Mother called out to ask if I wanted to go with them. Never able to make up my mind, I hesitated. Yes. No. Yes. No.

"We'll be back soon," she called again, getting into the car. But as I watched it back out of the drive and start slowly down the dusty street, a feeling of being left behind rose up in me strongly. I whirled around suddenly and took off after them, bare feet carrying me as fast as they could, hair, tears, and snot streaming. I kept hollering at the top of my lungs that I did want to go, did want to go, did want . . .

When the car finally stopped, about half a block away, Grandma opened her door and leaned forward, face set, eyes hard, to let me crawl in and huddle miserably on the back seat of the little coupe. Mother put the car in gear.

"Don't ever do anything like that again," she said sharply, and Grandma told me I'd made a public spectacle of myself. Then, they spoke in low, hushed tones to each other for the rest of the ride, leaving me alone to nurse my shame in solitude.

I had ruined their little lark to the country, ruined their afternoon. I had ruined the game I'd been enjoying, ruined the fun. I had ruined everything, and no one would ever love me again.

Moments Passed

jd young

I cry for moments passed

Those meant for me to enjoy
And I should have accepted

Those that hurt someone
And I knew when it happened

Those I chose not to appreciate
And became more stubborn

Those that were received badly
And I should have known

Those that offered comfort
And I ignored

Those that sat on my lips
And I did not allow to leave

Those that may have healed
And I kept so very silent

Those that caused mayhem
And I enjoyed the moment

Those that I cannot take back
And haunt me daily

In Three Minutes

Jack Daily

What can you do in three minutes? In three minutes of the final round of a title fight, you could score a knockout and become heavyweight champion of the world. Your peers would be household names like George Foreman, Muhammad Ali, and Joe Frazier. Wear the belt proudly.

The Kentucky Derby is billed as the most exciting two minutes in sports. Post time is the first Saturday in May. The extra minute after the winner crosses the finish line gives you time to tear in half all the losing tickets, toss them high in the air like New Year's Eve confetti, and head to the bar for a mint julep.

Maybe we will never win a heavyweight title or be in Churchill Downs for the Running of the Roses, but the mint julep is certainly within reason.

Stretch three to four minutes, and you can poach an egg. Serve the egg with creamed spinach in Béchamel sauce topped with warm asparagus and hollandaise, and you have eggs Sardou. An extra minute to go from cook to chef seems worth the wait.

Change the Record, Will You

Jack Daily

When I was fourteen, I got my first record player. With its shiny green plastic base and hinged lid, it was portable and automatic. You could load several, lightweight 45 RPM records on its spindle, and as it finished one recording, the next disc would drop onto the turntable. Vinyl spinning on vinyl was not particularly good for preservation, but I could listen to uninterrupted music for nearly thirty minutes. If I wanted to create a playlist beginning with the Five Satin's "In the Still of the Night" followed by the Coaster's "Young Blood," I simply loaded the spindle in that order. I thought the world was headed in the right direction.

My parents, on the other hand, had to contend with heavier vinyl—the sixteen-inch diameter disc that spun at 78 RPM. They listened to Frank Sinatra, Patti Page, Perry Como, and all the big bands of the day. Their record collection was held in the base of the same four-foot-long cabinet that contained the turntable, with wooden separators to keep the records upright. If one of their monolithic discs fell over, it would most likely break into pieces. The cabinet also came with a built-in AM radio. AM was the dominant type of station on the airways. But I could listen to radio on-the-go with my silver-plastic transistor radio that also included an FM tuner. Whether it was Tall Paul spinning R&B or Tommy Charles for the new Pop sounds, I was in touch.

By the 1960s and into my college days, the recording industry's players and media technology had advanced. Most record players could still support the 45's, but the spindle was now detachable. The new format was the Long Play (LP) album. It was still analog vinyl and turned at a remarkably slow 33 1/3 RPM. One side of an LP could play several songs with a total play length of 45 minutes or so. The other treat was the artwork on the album cover. Maybe the kids in middle school during the second decade of the 21st century would not recognize the lads of Liverpool, but everyone else on the planet would recognize them crossing the white-striped asphalt of London's Abbey Road. The other change that occurred during this era was globalization—before it was popular to use the term. Kids in Asia, Europe, North America and every other continent were listening to the same music. Okay, maybe not in Antarctica.

The next wave of change occurred in the 1970s and was spawned by the versatility and small-form factor of magnetic tape as launched by the audio cassette and the short-lived 8-track player, primarily used in cars of the day. But this change was a setback. We lost the artwork, and if the cassette was mistakenly left on the dashboard of your car during a summer day, we lost the entire album.

In the 1980s the digital revolution began with the nearly indestructible polycarbonate plastic of the compact disc. And we got the artwork back, although on a much smaller scale. The CD had staying power, and national chains like Tower Records spread across the country. These large stores had rows of neatly ordered CDs but still carried their vinyl counterparts. The salespeople knew their music. If you liked an artist or new genre, they could point you toward other music you might like, and they looked cool with their pink spiked hair.

Everything has changed again. Tower Records has closed its doors, but you can still buy CDs at generic hubs like Wal-Mart and Target. Just don't expect to have a conversation about music or to be offered suitable alternative choices. But this, too, is quickly giving way to Amazon, Google, and Apple stores conveniently located in the nearest cloud. You can download, upload, stream, and purchase almost any music you want. There are Genius generated playlists of iTunes and Apple's SIRI, an artificial intelligent assistant who may suggest a new song if asked.

Are things better? I don't know. As Alfred North Whitehead once observed, "The art of progress is to preserve order amid change and to preserve change amid order." I can't think of a better example than the transitions in the way we buy, store, and listen to music.

Watercolor: © Nancy O'Connor

Life of Tides
a villanelle
Sophi Link

Editor's Note: The highly structured villanelle is a nineteen-line poem with two repeating rhymes and two refrains. The form is made up of five tercets followed by a quatrain. The first and third lines of the opening tercet are repeated alternately in the last lines of the succeeding stanzas; then in the final stanza, the refrain serves as the poem's two concluding lines.

Let the tide sweep your worries away

In the soft-washed light of ending day.

Live by the moon's gentle sway.

Smile for the laughter of yesterday

But live in the love that reigns today,

And let the tide sweep your worries away.

Simmer in the sun's red-burned rays
As they sink beneath an indigo wave;
Live by the moon's gentle sway.

Lose yourself in the splashing spray,
Admire the smoke as it starts to fade,
And let the tide sweep your worries away.

It's times like these that I would pray.
If I had a God, then I would say
Let me live by the moon's gentle sway.

Under the stars' fractured display
This is your decision day.
Just let the tide sweep your worries away
And live by the moon's gentle sway.

Photograph: © Diane Burdette

A Glow From Within

Diane Burdette

Like most immigrants of the early 1900s, Helen took her place in the melting pot of America. The feisty, strong-willed woman decided to leave her home in Budapest and sail toward a better life. The young woman had lost two children during infancy and was determined to find happiness. After transitioning into a new country, she and her husband Michael found work in menial jobs. They were hard workers and saved whatever they could. I have to wonder if this was the land of promise she had dreamed about. Were her dreams ever fulfilled?

Perhaps the cherubs sitting upon her grave may hold the answers to these questions. Once beautiful statues, they were left there like gargoyles protecting a solemn and serene place. Now, their presence harkens back to a different time. Their faces appear dirty, cracked, and broken. Sponge-like patterns of lichen have formed over their bodies from decades at the site.

Maybe her time on this planet was not all hardship and toil, for she was blessed with more children. Helen gave birth to four sons. Helen and Michael had acquired a small home, and for a while, it seemed as though luck was on her side. Michael loved to work with his hands and added a small porch with gingerbread trim. Helen spent many afternoons there, rocking her babies to sleep. When their father Michael came home, they would all gather around the radio. The young couple would listen to their favorite tunes and dance around the parlor. Helen loved to dance. Despite her short, stocky build, she was extremely light on her feet. People often remarked that when she danced, her eyes sparkled, and she seemed to glow from within. For just an instant, Helen felt carefree. The problems of the day would drift away. It seemed as though everything was falling into place.

Suddenly tragedy spread across this country. The Great Depression left families destitute, including Helen's. Work was scarce, and bread lines were long. Somehow, though, this family endured, and eventually her prayers were answered. Michael found work as a carpenter.

Michael was a diligent worker. He was content to labor from dawn to dusk, as long as he was able to provide for his family. After several months at the job, a horrible accident occurred. A large beam fell on Michael and pinned him to the ground. His leg was badly injured and an amputation was necessary. For the first time, Michael found himself dependent upon the matriarch of the family. He was a proud man, raised with Old World values. Now, the happiness was gone from his eyes, and his demeanor changed forever. Helen found work in a kitchen and supported the family as well as she could. Many years passed, and her boys grew into strong men. They began to prosper and went out to start their own families. Meanwhile, Michael's health was deteriorating. He grew weaker and weaker and slipped away from Helen's world. Helen had a real sense of emptiness. For the first time in her life, she was alone.

Helen did adapt to being on her own. She led a very modest life, but there were happy moments too. A visit from her sons would always raise her spirits, and her grandchildren brought a smile to her face.

Eventually, the little home became shabby, gray, and in disrepair, almost reflecting her worn appearance. When she could no longer manage, she had to rely on others for care. Her golden years were spent in isolation until the time of her passing.

Now her residence, though vacant for years, occasionally glows from within. A translucent figure emerges from behind the sheer curtains. Is it an unsettled spirit in search of a former life? Or could it be something else? The cherubs may know, but for now, they are silent.

Surviving Auschwitz
Bobbie Troy

when the guards removed my clothes

they thought they took my soul

but I managed to hide it

in an invisible pocket

when night came

I retrieved my soul

From its hiding place

and used it like a blanket

to cover

my naked, starving, dying body

Originally published 11/9/2010, the 72nd anniversary of Kristallnacht, on vox poetica: http://poemblog.voxpoetica,com/2010/11/10/surviving-auschwitz.aspx

Bedtime

Nancy Scott

When I was a little girl and Mother put me to bed, she'd sometimes take the top sheet—real cotton muslin, not a modern blend—and snap it high in the air, then let it billow over me like a cloud. She always laughed when she did this, and it seemed to give her such pleasure that I never said how much I disliked the flying lint getting in my eyes and up my nose, sticking to my lips.

Mother and I never got along when I was growing up. She was domineering, and I was rebellious. But now that I'm old and ill, I'd give anything for that woman to come into my lonely bedroom, snatch up the top sheet and shake it above me, then let it settle like a blessing, before she tucked it in and made me safe for the night.

No More Sad Songs

Jack Daily

If I could be in charge for a day, the sound of music would change forever. Long ago we had well-behaved notes with easy-to-remember names like *A*, *B*, and *C*. And then some crazy musician decided these notes were not good enough.

"No," he said. "We need sharps and flats."

So he anointed a *C* sharp and a *C* flat and wasn't done until all the other notes had these ill-fitting additions. So the unpretentious and quite wholesome *C* got two half-note, dim-witted cousins he never wanted.

I'm sure there are some long-haired, rock-and-roll guitar players; pot-smoking jazz musicians; and shiftless country stars singing sad songs who are quite fond of *C*'s renegade cousins. But ask yourself, why are there so many people who can't carry a tune and always sing off key?

Of course, it's because of all those damn sharps and flats.

When I am in charge, it will be illegal for anyone to play music with these half-tone aberrations. Everyone will be able to sing on key. History will record a significant achievement.

The Old Age Repository
Bobbie Troy

Wake up, Grandma. We're here.

Huh, huh? Oh, ya mean the old age repository?

Grandma, please. It will be okay. You'll see. Look how pretty is it up there on the hill.

I still can't believe yur doin' this ta me, Sonny. I practically raised ya up. Now yur dumpin' me off like so much garbage. That's all I am ta ya? Okay, Okay. Have it yur way. Get on home now. At least ya've still got a home ta go ta.

Granny, we went over all this. Look at your leg. It's broken in five places. If I hadn't stopped by your place after work, you'd be dead by now. I just couldn't leave you alone any more.

Yeah, well. Maybe dead is better than dumped.

§ § §

Hi, Mr. Johnson. Before you go up to see your grandmother, I would like to talk to you. Please come into my office.

Thank you, Doctor. What is it? Is Grandma okay? Does she like it here? She can be stubborn if she sets her mind against something.

Well, she's okay. Physically, that is. But mentally she's having a hard time adjusting. She's aloof, and well, I'm afraid she's retreated into another reality. That's fairly common with newcomers to our facility. But she should get over it in time and adjust perfectly fine. So for now, just go along with whatever she says.

Yes, Doctor, I guess you know best. But I really don't know what you're talking about.

§ § §

Hi, Grandma. Your room looks nice with all your pictures out. I brought you some candy. Grandma, aren't you going to say hi?

Why should I? I'm busy. We're outta control. Spinnin' outta orbit. I'm tryin' ta reach mission control to redirect our flight path, but nobody answers. So I have ta keep tryin'. Mission control, mission control, this is Granny123. Do ya read me? Do ya read me? I repeat, this is Granny123. Come in, mission control.

Look, just leave the candy, Sonny. I don't have time fur ya right now.

But Grandma, I came to visit all the way from the city. You know how long that takes. I want to make sure you're happy here. How's the food? Have you made any friends?

Mission control, mission control. Do ya read me? This is Granny123. I repeat, this is Granny123. Come in, mission control.

Grandma, stop this nonsense. This isn't a spaceship. It's the Hillview Old Age Home. You know that. Now stop being silly. You know I love you, but I had no choice.

I don't know nuthin' but this is an old-age repository that's outta orbit an' outta control. Just flingin' out space garbage every day. One comes in, one goes out. Garbage in, space garbage out. Nothin' more, Sonny. But when I get control, I'm gonna aim this baby at all the houses of all the relatives that dumped their loved ones in this old-age repository. A smart meteor. That's what it 'ill be. A smart meteor that self-destructs after it's done the job. Then none of us 'ill have nuthin' to worry about.

Mission control, mission control, this is Granny123. Do ya read me?

Originally published June 20, 2011 on Jeanette Cheezum's Cavalcade of Stars: http://cavalcadeofstars.wordpress.com/2011/06/20/bobbie-troy/.

Love's Spell

*"That love is all there is,
is all we know of love."
-Emily Dickinson*

The following section will take you into the reality of expressing heartfelt desires.

Drawing: © Isabelle Anctil

Isabelle's Cowboy
Caryn Moya Block

Isabelle stood at the gas pump filling up her car when the young cowboy appeared. He stood before her, and she was caught. Her eyes slowly perused his perfect form, from the tip of his cowboy boots, to the leather chaps tied around his legs, to his huge shiny belt buckle, to the leather jacket and finally to the tan cowboy hat that he wore. His tall form and broad shoulders only added to the image.

What a fine figure of a man, she thought. But then she glanced down at her age-spotted hands and saw the reflection of her silver hair in the shiny surface of the gas pump. Well, damn, she thought. The only way she could have this cowboy was if she adopted him. But then, she smiled as she lost a little piece of her heart to the tall cowboy. Because falling in love at the gas pump reminded her that she was still alive and kicking. As she got in her car and drove away, she wondered what brought a "real" cowboy to Orange County, Virginia.

The Cowboy

Jan Settle

Hank leaned against his truck with his thumbs hooked in his belt loops, gazing up at the morning light filtering through the tall shade trees. Of all the states he'd passed through on the rodeo circuit, he thought, Virginia surely must be one of the prettiest. The warm summer breeze had a mild, sweet fragrance that he'd never smelled back home in Texas. He had a good feeling about this town, this rodeo.

He headed into the gas station; it was time to get this day started with a morning cup o' Joe. He had a full day ahead of him at the local ranch. Well, he guessed they call them "farms" here in Virginia. He chose the tallest cup and started pouring the dark liquid energy when something like a bright bolt of silver light caught his eye. Gazing up, he saw a tall, slender woman dressed in denim. Her face was like a soft rose petal, her hair sparkled like the finest silver from the mines in Mexico. Her most striking feature was her eyes, blue as the big skies out West. He was stunned by their intensity.

"Howdy, ma'm," he said, catching her attention.

"Good morning!" was her reply, voice as smooth as honey.

"Beautiful morning!" he said, wishing he could have come up with something more original.

"Yes, it is!" she agreed.

As she turned to walk out the big glass door, he hesitated. Should he follow her out? Engage her in more small talk, find out more about her? Before he could make a move, the cashier ran up his coffee tab and asked for $2.59. He paid the man and left hurriedly, wildly scanning the parking lot for her. She was gone.

Hank climbed into his truck, bothered by his missed opportunity. Still, he had a sense that he would see her again. Maybe he'd get a chance to show her his roping and riding skills at the rodeo, or maybe she'd come back to the gas station to tank up. He had missed this chance, but he wouldn't let it happen again.

He reached up and pulled down the brim of his cowboy hat to shield his eyes from the bright morning sun. The rodeo circuit could be tiring and lonesome, but on this day, in this little Virginia town, there was hope in his heart.

He Would Wait

Judith Dreyer

She said,

While sipping

White wine,

Sitting

Arms crossed,

Head banded

Lungs caught

Between hope

And despair,

In the café

Across the street

Where they first met,

Eyes watered,

Hands clenched,

And she thought

I cannot cry again

And flung the words

Trapped in her heart,

Covered in ice

That cracked her voice,

"How could you leave me

Then come back again?"

He said,

While gulping a beer

Sitting

Arms held forward

Groping, meeting

Her hands

Across the table

In the café

Not far from

Where they began

Heart taut

But not for naught

For he's worked

Out the kinks

Between heart and mind

So she'd understand.

He had to let go

So they both could grow

Though years slipped away

He thought

Now is always okay,

"To start over and begin again."

She said,

As a tear slipped past

Resolve and certainty

Began to crack

The wall across her hope

That couldn't expand

In a breath or two

The hurt traveled deep

And trust went awry.

You stayed away

I cried

Your name every day, and choked,

"How can I love you again?"

He said,

As a tear slipped past

And thought of

No one else

Over the miles

That passed

Roots were shown

Where he belonged

He began to dig

And plant till the

Trunk grew straight

And the limbs bent

So he could carry her

To his heart

To melt the band he placed

From the start.
Would she hear him and trust again?
Give us another chance
It's time.
He thought, then whispered,
"Because I simply love you."

He wiped away the tears
His and hers
And sat back
To wait like a single seed
That under concrete
Finds the sun
Thrives
Though
A hundred years go by.
He didn't mind.
He would wait.

Merry Christmas, My Love
Bobbie Troy

I look over my shoulder

and another year has passed

without you

I gently wipe the

newly fallen snow

from your grave

and whisper

into the cold morning air

Merry Christmas, My Love

Originally published 12/24/2009 on www.voxpoetica.com:
http://poemblog.voxpoetica.com/2009/12/24/merry-christmas-my-love.aspx.

Pretense

Bobbie Troy

pretense

hung in the air

like the uneven shadow

of an old apple tree

that put distance between

what she wanted to say

and he wanted to hear

and between

what he wanted to say

and she wanted to hear

Drawing: © Nancy O'Connor

An Unexpected Pleasure
Caryn Moya Block

Lord Raine, Earl of Greymare, sat with his head on the table and snored. He could hear the raucous party going on around him. The doctored wine Lord Daegal thought he had stolen from the peddler was doing its work. Daegal's penchant for fine wine would prove to be his downfall. Soon, the entire household would be asleep.

Raine stretched out his arm and mumbled, pushing his glass of wine onto the floor. He heard the three large dogs that roamed the hall lapping it up greedily. The dogs would soon be one more obstacle out of the way. Everything was going according to plan.

Raine and his men had sneaked into Daegal's hall to rescue Raine's younger brother, Avery, from the dungeon. In order to forego bloodshed, they had decided to engage in a game of trickery.

Slitting his eyes, Raine saw his second-in-command, Lord Sherard, nod his head. This was their signal that the other men were in position and that a jug of wine had been delivered to the guards in the dungeon. Now, it was a waiting game. Raine closed his eyes and continued to act as if he were sleeping.

He felt a slight figure worm her way under his arm and press close to his body.

"I know who you are, Your Grace, even with your disguise. I know that you've come for your brother. Never fear, I have no intention of giving away your cause."

Raine cracked his eyes open and reached for his dagger. He would prefer to save his brother without killing anyone, but if necessary, no one would stand in his way. The woman at his side was a mere slip of a girl and appeared to be a servant.

"I beg of you, Sir. Save my mistress, Lady Catherine. She is a great heiress and cousin to Lord Daegal. He holds her prisoner in her room and is starving her. Once she is too weak to fight, he will send his friend Lord Faren in to rape her and then wed her, so he can claim her properties."

Raine could hear the sincerity in the woman's voice. He didn't need another problem to add to this caper. But could he in good conscience leave a woman in Daegal's clutches?

"Very well. You have a quarter-hour to gift her guards with a jug of wine from the three casks Daegal has stolen. Then, come back here to me. If you are late, I will leave without you and your lady."

Raine lifted his head and saw Sherard moving toward them. He shook his head no as he yawned and mumbled. The servant girl disappeared into the kitchens below. Raine knew she would be quick to follow his orders. He lay down on the bench and pretended to snore some more.

As the noise in the banquet hall started to change to more snores than laughter, Raine rolled off the bench and crouched close to the floor. Daegal and the others at the head table appeared to be passed out, as were the men-at-arms at the table near the door. Raine caught Sherard's eye and gave the signal to proceed.

Raine had brought his five best knights with him. He knew at his signal that Brant and Ryce would be freeing his brother from the dungeon. Kenton and Selwyn would be dropping the drawbridge and readying the horses. Sherard would relay his signal, then cover Raine's back. The men worked well together and were more a family than a fighting unit.

Raine started moving toward the stairway leading up to the family chambers. If Lady Catherine was being held in her room, it would be up these stairs. He was glad to see the servant girl making her way to him. She slipped under his shoulder, appearing to hold him up as he performed a drunken weave through the sleeping crowd and up the stairs.

Once at the top of the stairs and out of sight of the downstairs hall, Raine straightened. He motioned the girl to proceed him and followed her around a corner. He smiled as he saw two guards slumped on the floor. He reached down and removed the key ring from the guard's belt. The keys rattled on the ring as he tried to unlock the door. Raine was surprised when the sound of breaking crockery was heard on the other side of the door.

"Daegal, if you come into this room I will cut your little black heart from your chest," shouted a feminine voice.

Raine looked down at the serving girl in question, but she just smiled and shrugged her shoulders.

"Lady Catherine, it's me Maud. I have brought Lord Raine to rescue you."

"Thank God, come quickly then," Catherine said.

Raine finally found the right key, and the door swung open. He walked in to see a vision in a blue gown. Her porcelain skin gleamed in the candlelight. Her long russet curls looked like flames licking at her skin. She stood proudly at the end of the bed, a dagger in her right hand while her left hand clutched the bed post.

"Maud, get the bag under the bed with my things," Catherine directed.

Raine watched as she put the dagger away on her belt. But when she tried to take a step away from the bed, she wavered and almost fell.

"Damnation, woman! You are ill," Raine said as he grasped her around the waist and supported her.

"Not ill, Your Grace, just weak from hunger and lack of sleep," Catherine said.

Raine held her carefully, not wanting to injure her. Now that he was close to her, he could see the circles under her eyes and feel the tremors running through her. He knew Daegal was a villain. He should have killed him after all.

Hearing footsteps in the hallway Raine looked up to see Sherard enter the room. Sherard faltered, then smiled. He was such a lady's man, the pretty one in their bunch. He had constantly encouraged Raine to take a woman of his own.

"Your brother Avery is free, and we must be away. What treasure is this?" asked Sherard.

A fierce feeling of protectiveness gripped Raine.

"This is My Lady Catherine. Get her bag from Maud. Maud fetch my lady a cloak. We must be off."

Raine swept Catherine up into his arms. She felt fragile and small. Then he ran down the stairs and out to the courtyard. He sheltered the lady close to his heart, keeping her safe. There could still be a guardsman left awake to challenge them. He saw his men with the horses and breathed a sigh of relief. The only noises coming from the gatehouse were snores.

Taking a quick inventory, Raine made sure his men were all accounted for. Avery appeared pale and thin but was sitting on his horse with determination.

"Sherard, give Kenton the bag and then hand Lady Catherine up to me. You will take Maud up with you. The Dwale Potion, that was in the wine, will last only another hour or so. We must be in Sherwood Forest by daylight."

Raine mounted his horse and leaned down to take Catherine into his arms. He folded her cloak around her, keeping her nestled close to his chest. She smiled as her eyes drifted shut. When Maud was mounted safely behind Sherard, Raine gave the signal, and they were riding hard across the bailey.

Raine looked down at the sleeping woman in his arms. Rescuing her was going to cause a horrendous amount of trouble. Daegal would never willingly give up such a wealthy prize. But he wouldn't have changed a thing. Catherine was everything he was looking for in a mate. He felt his heart recognize her.

Catherine needed rest and food as quickly as possible. Raine smiled when she nestled closer in her sleep. He wanted her. He wanted her happiness and her safety. It was time for the Earl of Greymare to take a wife. An audience with the king was in order, and then a visit with the Archbishop of Canterbury. No one would take Catherine away from him now that he had found her.

Unrequited

Marlee Laws

Ripples from above

The stone cold face of a lover

Mystic fallen for perfection

Sea breeze tails

Shining and frothing in the deep

Breathless breathing beneath the waves

Tentative kiss

Hard cheek and still eyes unmoving

Gentle fingers frozen to a stone blade

Only one dead

Feelings unrequited and stale

But persistence

Destiny

jd young

My heart breaks in squares,
triangles, and magnificent iridescent pieces.

He said he loved me more than life,
then his being ended.

I am left reviewing the iridescent
spots he insisted made my life worthwhile.

He encouraged my every breath to make a
difference; he made me relevant.

He consumed my soul.

Now, I must act to ensure our next
meeting matters and fulfills our destiny.

Relative Madness
Sophi Link

Darkness inspires relative madness,
and in the dark I unfolded your ribs
to melt my heart to yours like plastic.
Your eyes illustrate my subconscious.

I would like to be your hummingbird
To fly across fields of flower tops
And sing through zigzagged worlds
before pausing in your palm a moment.

You are the shadow that I sculpted,
the shadow built from shades of dreams
unfurled from that celestial cerebrum
where reality holds no power to persuade.

If reality were real enough to realize me,
I might admit that I don't know you,
but if I can fool myself that I love you,
this mad night will listen to me ramble.

Finding Love Again

Judith Dreyer

I'm sitting here at the winery, in the tasting room that overlooks the vineyard, while gray clouds fill the sky and hide the sunset. Dozens of birds flit through the trees, strut through the grassy field, and fly through the vineyard, leaving spots of seed-filled bird poop everywhere. I have cleaned the tables and chairs on the outside deck twice in the short time I've been here, while enjoying the afternoon haze and unusually mild temperatures.

I can't help thinking that my life has a romantic flavor to it. Here I am in a vineyard, quiet and stately, that awaits winter's coming and going so it can bloom again. Clouds pass by and keep the air mild, though the sun goes down as if behind closing doors. The tasting room, clean and orderly, waits for a holiday shopper. Evening slowly pulls down the shades of the day, as I sit and read a novel while waiting for the owners to return from errands. The owners have the room ready for their family's Christmas celebration, which is only a few days away. Petit Verdot, Vidal Blanc, once lovely grapes on a vine now transformed into wine, fill the shelves near me. Here I am in a lovely quaint setting. A romantic one, too, as soft illuminations both inside and out light my heart in this place where I have landed.

As I sit in the silence here, I have a feeling of love being reborn within touching places that have rusty-and-oxidized chains and locked doors that still remain. I feel something in this gentle evening that seems to softly rattle those chains and jimmy the doors. It seems as if a golden thread from love's source seeps through the cracks under doors and through keyholes, finding its way in somehow no matter how I resist. How this happens I cannot tell you, but hope enters and catches me off guard this evening. I feel softness, a tenderness stirs in my heart, reaching places I thought hopelessly blocked. I feel the breath of love in the wind. It caresses my cheek touching me. I sense romance in the air tonight, too. Ironic isn't it? It seems as if I needed to feel love heal and then stir within me in this magical silence, before I can open to love again. There is no man by my side as I close up the tasting room and head home; no one is there to greet me when I open the door to my home. Yet it is love I capture in my beating heart that I will hold close as the chains rust away so I can reopen the doors to love again.

First published at calvacadeofstars@wordpress.com on 2/28/2012

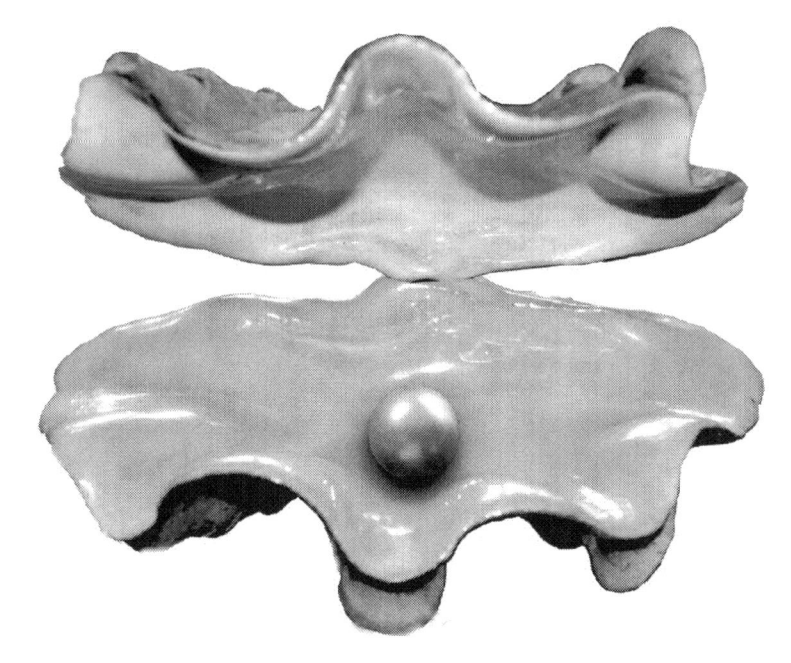

Digital Collage: © Jeanne Tanks

Pearl

Pennie L. Kinsey

I likened love
To a pearl within its shell
That I patiently waited
To gently open
Of its own accord

Love's Spell

And then, I beheld

Its spirit, its very soul

In the brilliant sphere

Beginning to unfold

No current was strong enough

To dislodge the opulent

Globe

From its resting place

Yet,

As I reached out

For the shell

And picked it up

The pearl rolled

Softly into my hands

And,

I have kept it near my heart

Ever since

My Love

jd young

I sit here tonight—to my side is a screened, open window.
I hear crickets. A street light from two roads over flickers at my side.
The radio is playing, but I hear only the soft breeze
pushing through the curtains.
It is quiet. So very quiet. I am happy it is not humid.
Almost pleasant tonight.
I sit waiting for a love that will never appear.
I sit at the ready should he surprise me.
It was a long ago time, he crept to my window,
tapped 'til I opened the screen and we kissed.
Short, quick kisses. I was young, and
he was afraid my father would find us.
The light in the window is dim,
that pinkish tone that happens when street lights get old.
I can feel the quiet. The dog that howls is far away.
The moon is only half tonight, but it is measurable.
So many nights I sit and wait.
Many nights I feel the darkness.
Many nights I yearn for that warm touch.
Many nights I hope.
Many nights fear covers my soul.
So many nights I wait.
Always.

Drawing: © Kathy Webber

That Day
Jack Daily

We walked on sun-sparkled sand
Smiling, thinking,
holding each other's gaze.
The hours pushed the tide away.

We laughed, as you cried wet tears
of joy into my stories.
Footprints casting memories
along the way,
it was a witty day that day.

Previously published on vox poetica.

Plowed Under
Gwen Monohan

Icy sheets of leftover snow
Glow with a gray sheen
Like a level expanse of cloudy sea.

After the foamy sky clears
To a faded winter blue,
I'll still send for you with memories.

Our shiny beach house—barn
Hovers low in frosty air, rising
Dune-like to face our gleaned horizon.

Secure atop waves of frozen stubble
From last year's matted corn,
We channel spring's tide promise.

Previously published on vox poetica.

We'll Meet When It's Right
Judith Dreyer

Did you know it was the trees that sent you to me?
Did you know it was my whisper the wind carried to you?
Did you know it was the stone under your knee
That poked and said she's coming?
Did you know it was the scent of the rose
That told you I was here?

Did you know your flowers would capture
my heart as they hold yours?
Did you know the sun and the clouds watch over us
as hawks dance in the sky?
Did you know the moon weaves her beams
through the stars and our nights?
Did you know the heavens move our paths
to join though we know not the why?

I know you not in this moment.
I see you not in my heart but in the wisps of night
I feel you, though in my knowing
And trust we will meet when it is right.

2/28/2012: Published at *calvacadeofstars@wordpress.com*

Feeding the Creative Fires

Food has always been a source of inspiration. Here it is a source of sneaky revenge, happy marriages, friendship, family traditions, international travel, and holiday stress. Bon Appétit!

Photograph: © Caryn Block

Tails From the Sea

D.J. Christiano

She sat down at the dining room table, the same table she had sat around a thousand times. Memories flooded her mind as she remembered her parents' joy during holiday meals as they watched their three grandchildren take part in family traditions and celebrate happy milestones. She also remembered the tears as they gathered around the same table to mourn the loss of those grandparents and how family meals helped heal the wounds of life's heart-stabbing moments. It all had happened here, at this table where she now sat. Those memories were a part of the past. The present was a far different situation. This time, she sat alone, all alone in this huge house, except for the precious memories now dearer than she could ever have imagined. Now, she sat for the last time at this table, waiting for the movers to come.

She sat for what seemed to be an eternity and finally called the moving company. The dispatcher said the moving truck had been stuck in traffic and was now on the way. That was nearly an hour ago, and it was getting late. She had not had anything to eat since early morn. The emotions of the day had stolen her appetite, just as this move was stealing her heart. Her head was starting to ache to match the aching in her back. Packing up the things she was to take had been exhausting. She decided she could wait no longer and called her favorite Chinese take-out to order shrimp, rice, and eggrolls. She was the only one in the family who liked Chinese food, and since she was the only one eating dinner, she felt this was a logical choice. She sat in the dining room again to guess who would ring the doorbell first, the food-delivery person or the movers. In reality, it didn't matter.

Her cell phone rang. Its eerie echo broke the silence she had experienced during the day. It seemed that another hour would pass before the movers arrived. They had had a long day, and the driver decided to stop for dinner. She was very glad she had ordered her dinner as well. Just as the phone call ended, the doorbell rang. Her food had arrived. She paid for the delivery, brought the food to the table and began the last meal she would have in the same dining room that held her precious memories.

The dining room had been newly decorated last year at her husband's insistence. He had told her the room was old and drab. It had served them well, but he felt it needed an update with fresh new paint to brighten and liven up the space. At times, she had wondered if he was discussing the room or "her." He said he had met a decorator, one with a lively personality and new ideas. He asked his wife to meet with the decorator and listen to her suggestions. She did, just listen, that is. The only thing that was agreed upon was keeping the beautiful chandelier that was purchased during her honeymoon trip. It was exquisite, one of a kind, hand-made of lead crystal. The store owner said she and her husband could have it for half price. The owner was selling his shop and wanted to decrease his inventory. The honeymooners explained they were newlyweds and didn't even have a home yet. They left with the chandelier and the anticipation of someday being able to afford their dream home.

As time went on, new homes were purchased that had their own chandeliers. During each move, the crystal chandelier was taken down and hung in the new home. This home where she sat was to be their final purchase; their dream home was a reality. The address read Country Club Drive, prime real estate, the realtor told them. It had been their home for over twenty years.

Now it was over. Her life had changed. The children were in college or had graduated. She was soon to become the ex-wife, and the decorator would become the new Mrs. The wife's attorney had told her it would be a mistake to ask for the house in the divorce settlement. In a few years she would not be able afford it. Take what he is willing to give you; buy a condo and move on. The judge will look favorably on that and maybe give you a little more alimony. She remembered the words "give you" as if she had not done the work of three by raising children and taking care of family matters for twenty-eight years. "Give you, indeed." Against her better judgment, she decided to take the settlement and not put up a fight for more, even though she felt she was entitled.

Now, it was she who sat alone eating her Chinese meal, waiting for the movers. Her mood changed as the meal ended. She decided that indeed she was going to deal with this, move on to a new phase of her life and be happy. After all, isn't the best revenge happiness?

She was cleaning up her cartons from dinner as she gazed at the chandelier for the final time. She looked down at the table to find the leftover shrimp tails and bits of cabbage from the eggrolls. No, she would not lower herself to do something so childish, but then again, what harm could this little prank cause? She carefully lowered some of the leftovers into the recesses of the chandelier and went through the house, doing the same to the other chandeliers that hung in the living room, kitchen, and even the ones in the master bedroom and bath. As the last leftovers were hidden in the chandeliers, the doorbell rang, and the movers started to load what furniture she would take.

It was over. The furniture was loaded on the van, and she was to meet the movers at the condo. No time to think about the stupid thing she had done. Oh well, not a problem. It would smell for a few days and then dissolve into dust; the same way her marriage had.

Some months later, a neighbor who lived next door called to see how she was doing. She explained she was very busy with her new job. She had landed a position as an editor, finally using the journalism degree that was put to the side as she raised the children.

Had she heard about the house and her ex-husband's new marriage? She said she was no longer interested in either.

Her neighbor did not listen to her words of "no interest" but went on to tell her about the strange smell that was in the house. A smell, that didn't want to go away despite cleaners, ozone treatments, new paint, odor absorbers or the installation of new carpeting. The ex-wife felt that maybe she should say something or maybe not. "How odd," were the only words she could utter.

Another few months passed. The same neighbor called again. Did she hear that the old house was now up for sale? This smell just would not go away, and the new wife was not happy and wanted to move. "How interesting," was the reply.

The next few months brought a myriad of calls from neighbors, friends and even the ex-wife's children. Did she know that the house had been reduced in price three times? Realtors would no longer list the house. The new Mrs. threatened to leave if she and her husband did not move. The smell was getting to her. "How very sad," was the reply to each remark. Each caller had asked if there was anything she could think of to solve this problem. She gave no reply to that query.

Her conscience was beginning to bother her. Should she call and confess or offer a suggestion about a thorough cleaning of light fixtures? Then, she had an idea. It might make everyone happy, especially her. She would offer to trade living spaces, her condo for the house. She called her ex. They both agreed. Her ex said to minimize losses, he was going to take all the furniture. She agreed. The publishing company she worked for had given her an advance for a book she wrote. She could definitely afford new furniture.

Moving day came once again. She arrived with the movers, turned the key to the house and expected an overwhelming smell to engulf her. The smell was just of a stuffy house. Nevertheless, armed with a heavy-duty cleaner, her first job would be to clean the chandeliers.

She went first into the dining room; no chandelier was present. She quickly ran to each room where she had placed her parting gifts. Not one chandelier remained. There was a note from her ex on the kitchen table apologizing for taking the chandeliers. He wanted them to remind himself of better times, and as soon as he got back on his financial feet, he would be placing them in his new home. He hoped they would bring him peace and good memories.

He also had left a book on the table—one she had forgotten when she moved out. She looked at the book. It was one of her favorites by Ann Morrow Lindbergh, a woman who had overcome the worst of all tragedies. She decided unpacking could wait until morning. Tonight she would order some Chinese and reread the book she held close to her heart, *A Gift from the Sea*.

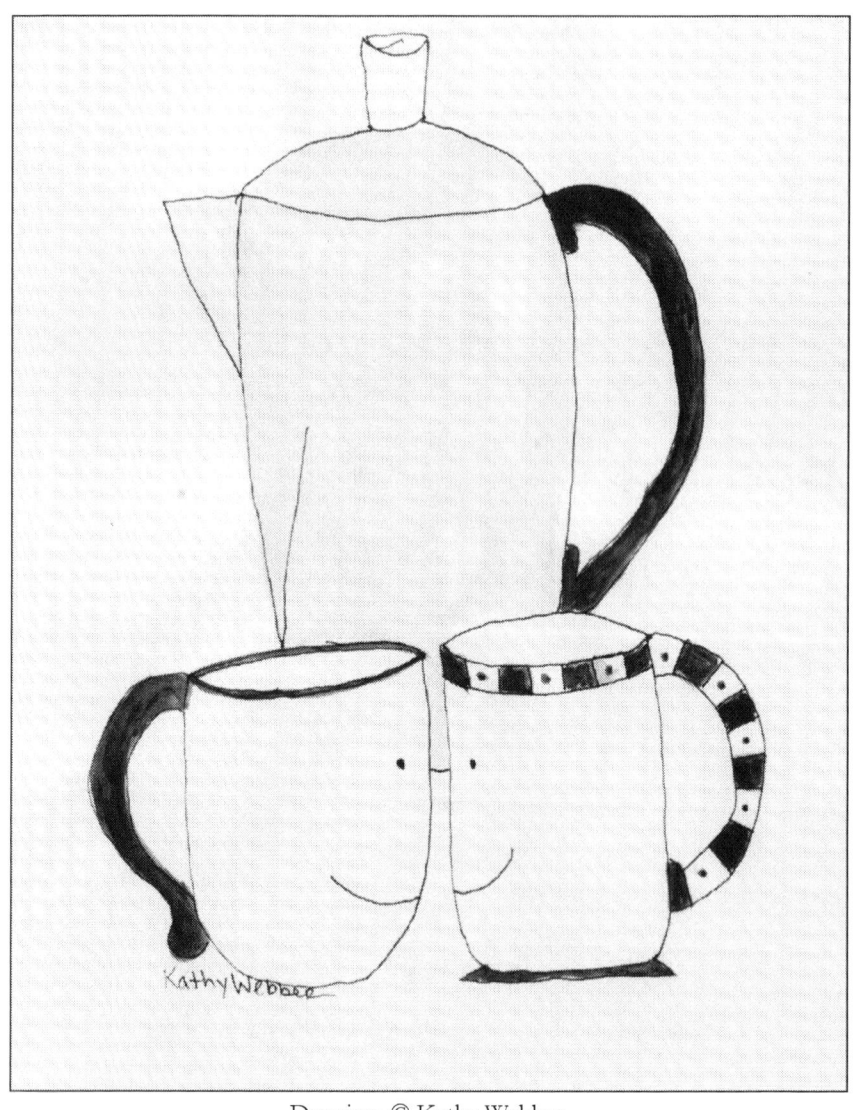

Drawing: © Kathy Webber

Dear Diane

Bobbie Troy

if you remember
i think it was in some strange court in tasmania
or maybe in your kitchen/our kitchen over coffee
that you took out your precious written thoughts

and pushed the sugar my way

if you remember
i think it was in your kitchen/our kitchen in the afternoon sunlight
that you let me see the back of your head/heart
and the reasons behind, the contacts with
all the things that didn't let you be free

and I got up to get the milk from the fridge

if you remember
i think it was in the middle of a fresh pot of coffee
after so many cups of instant
that we realized where we were in terms of each other
and what we were

and sometime during all that
you gave me a new coffee mug

Originally published 10/6/2009 on www.voxpoetica.com. Nominated by Annmarie Lockhart, editor, for the 2010 Pushcart Prize. To hear Bobbie read this poem, go to http://aliceshapiro.com/bobbietroy.html.

Advice To My Newly Married Son
Martha Orr Conn

When she's dropped two raw eggs on the kitchen floor,
    And the soufflé turned out no winner,
        Kindly words a husband can say
            Are, "Let's go out to dinner."

    But to her there are even sweeter words,
        These will make you truly bewitchin'.
    Insist, "You go ahead and get ready, dear.
        I'll clean up the kitchen!"

The Art of Pasta

Jack Daily

On a canvas called pasta, the chef uses a variety of noodles, toppings, seasonings, and colors to create edible art. The combinational possibilities could stump an MIT professor. There is no best pasta dish I've ever eaten. But to borrow a cliché on another topic, some are better than others. Today's pasta primavera may trump yesterday's spaghetti with marinara only to be defeated on a future day by angel hair topped with garlic shrimp. Who wouldn't want to referee these match-ups?

Pasta contorts itself into many shapes and sizes. We have linguini, penne, spaghetti, macaroni, tortellini, and fettuccini. I'm Irish. Can you imagine how many types of pasta a nice Italian boy in Rome or Tuscany's country setting could name?

These wonderful noodles can be politically correct. The vegan will rave over the most organically grown semolina, and then cast a disparaging glance when he asks, "What brand do you buy?" Pasta topped with tofu (not a fan) can satisfy the most serious fitness trainer or Weight Watcher enrollee. But pasta can take on a darker, decadent side. Go to the neighborhood café for lunch and order pasta marinara with Italian sausage lathered in parmesan cheese. Want to sink deeper in sin? Point to the baked lasagna, ask for a glass of red, and cancel your midafternoon appointments. You will need a nap.

French food is delicate, American cuisine gets to the point, and restaurants offer Greek salads, Spanish tapas, Indian tandoori, Middle Eastern baba ghanoush, Chinese Kung Pao chicken. If that's not enough, restaurants gain popularity by claiming a fusion of these flavors. I love the variety of today's choices at both market and bistro. But on my menu, pasta wins hands down. Oh, waiter!

A Family Favorite

Diane Burdette

Grab a cookbook
find the spot
Grandma creased
made a lot

Time to bake
something nice
Flour, sugar,
pinch of spice.

Crack an egg
use a beater
Raisins added;
even sweeter

Preheat oven
set the timer
Just like Grandma's
nothing finer.

Family recipe
made with care
Wonderful aroma
fills the air

Creamy frosting
utensils glide
Ready to cut
serve with pride!

Composite Photograph: © Jeanne Tanks

Open Some More Wine

Fran Cecere

December, 2010, and it was time for the annual writers' Christmas party. We had food, wine, fun, and great conversation. Fran brought the wine and her favorite corkscrew to open it. Several of the men used the corkscrew and commented on how well designed it was. At the end of the party, the corkscrew was gone. Fran felt that somehow it had ended up in someone's bag and had gone on an unplanned trip to his or her home. She immediately shot off an email to all the writers asking them to let her know if they found the opener.

The night of the party, Bette had come without her husband Steve. He was busy planning another big event. When Bette got home, she found the corkscrew wrapped in the towel she had used to cover her chili pot. She put the corkscrew on her kitchen counter with a note saying, "bring to the meeting," then went to bed.

In the morning, Bette's husband Steve woke up before her. He saw the corkscrew on the counter and thought the note was for him. He had a very important meeting that day with the French ambassador to the United States. Steve had put together a gift case of wine, some cheese, and special treats from Virginia that the ambassador was to take back to Paris with him. Steve thought the corkscrew was such a clever gift to add to the package and hoped he would remember to thank Bette that night.

After the party, the gifts were taken to the limousine by Henri, the assistant to the French ambassador. The group boarded their private plane and flew to Paris. Two days later, Steve remembered to thank Bette for leaving the corkscrew as a present for the ambassador. Only then did she learn what had happened. Bette told her husband that it was an old used corkscrew with no real value, but Fran really liked it. The thought crossed Steve's mind that this was a really awkward situation, but he didn't know what he could do about it.

Later that day, Steve received a beautiful note from the ambassador thanking him for the gifts. The ambassador commented on the wine and cheese and stated that if there was anything he could do for Steve, all he had to do was ask. At that suggestion, Steve called Henri. While they were talking about other things, Steve jokingly told Henri the story of the corkscrew, and Henri said he thought the return of the wine opener would be no problem at all. In about a week, Henri was scheduled to return to the Washington area, and he would contact Steve if he was able to bring back the old corkscrew.

When the Ambassador heard about the situation, he found it quite funny and sent Henri to the kitchen where the opener was in a drawer with about twenty other corkscrews. It would never be missed if it were returned to the United States. Henri put it into his carry-on luggage. That weekend Henri went to England to visit his girlfriend. They laughed about the story and used the opener on a bottle of expensive wine he had bought to celebrate their anniversary. Then he put the corkscrew back in his bag.

Henri flew first class on a commercial jet from England to New York City. He had a meeting that day with a company in the Big Apple. That night he ordered room service and uncorked the wine with the opener. When Henri thought about how many times the corkscrew had been used in the past two weeks, he laughed.

When Henri arrived at LaGuardia Airport and was going through security before boarding the flight to DC, the guard pulled Henri's bag out of the X-ray machine and opened it. He took out the corkscrew and tossed it into the bin of items that were not allowed on the flight. Henri was very upset. How was he going to explain to Steve that at the last minute he lost the corkscrew to security in New York City? Suddenly there was a lot of yelling, and Henri turned to see three security guards and their dog running toward two men who were fighting. The dog hit the bin with the confiscated items and knocked it over. Henri saw the corkscrew skitter across the floor toward him. Pretending to tie his shoes, he bent over, picked up the corkscrew, and deftly put it back into his carry-on luggage.

The next day, Henri handed off the opener to Steve, who enjoyed hearing all the stories of what had happened since they last met. Steve absentmindedly put the opener into his pocket and promptly forgot about it. Several days later, Steve got a call from his neighbor Phil. In the past year, Phil had been on a very strict diet and had lost seventy-five pounds. Now, he needed to attend a wedding in Nashville,

Tennessee, and he did not have a suit jacket that fit him. Steve did not hesitate to loan him his best jacket. When Phil arrived in Tennessee and was dressing for the wedding, he found the corkscrew in the pocket. During the reception, he ordered a vintage wine for the bride's table and opened the bottle with the corkscrew. Then, he gave a charming toast to the happy couple.

When Phil returned the jacket to Steve, he mentioned the corkscrew and how he used it. Steve immediately took it from his jacket pocket and put it on the counter. He put a note on it telling Bette to bring it to her writers' meeting. The first Tuesday of the next month Bette returned the corkscrew to Fran.

When Fran got home she turned to her husband Roy and said, "Bette gave me the opener back. She came up with some crazy story about the corkscrew traveling thousands of miles and opening expensive wines. Bette is such a great storyteller. I'd be willing to bet it went from Culpeper to Rixeyville and back, but that's about it. Someday I'll tell you the funny story she told me about our corkscrew. In the meantime, do you want some wine?"

Fran casually tossed the wine opener into the drawer where she always kept it and said, "We don't need this tonight. I've got a bottle of wine already open in the refrigerator."

So Much Ado

Jack Daily

The hand-painted,
designer glasses
suddenly appear—
just like last year.

Can it be that time?

Who's invited, and who's not?
Again we will agree, "Just dear friends,
but why must there be only eight?"

Who will sit next to whom?
And you said,
"Not boy, girl, boy, girl.
Remember John and Georgia,
before anyone knew?
I'll ask Mary;
She'll know what to do."

"Is Malbec okay, with sparkling to start?"
And the music. You told me,
"The music must be fresh, not so
traditional, and not as loud as last year."

And the food
It must be perfect.
It will be discussed.
"Oh, I hope we have a hit this year.
There's so much to do, and
so many things to go wrong."

A small smile turned your lips,
as you turned to me,
and quietly said,
"Let's go away this year,
something different than last year."

The hand-painted,
designer glasses
were returned.
On the top shelf they stare,
beautiful and unused.

Previously published on vox poetica.

On the Edge

These stories will take you on an imaginative journey into the minds of animals and people, and then you will end up in space.

It's A Miracle

Fran Cecere

What on earth or under the earth was that horrible smell! Jennie opened her eyes and then quickly closed them as the late morning sun burned into her brain. She managed to look down long enough to realize that Larry's foot was almost in her mouth. He lay sleeping upside down in the bed, and when she managed to push his putrid-smelling foot away from her face, her own foot brushed right under his nose. He snorted and then sneezed so loud Jennie was sure he would wake the dead.

Jennie pushed him, and he rolled over and scratched his crotch. "Wake up you scumbag," she shouted.

He reached up and grabbed her arm. He brought her close to him and let out an extremely long burp.

Jennie laughed and then produced a long, loud belch of her own. "Top that one, loser," she said as the noise ended.

For several minutes, they each burped and tried to outdo one another. Then Larry passed the noisiest gas. "Oh, great," Jennie screamed, "the homerun of gross actions: stinky feet, belching, passing wind, and scratching. I think I should call the world news on this one."

As the rancid odor filled the room, Jennie jumped out of bed. She suddenly fell to the floor and found that her feet were tangled in the legs of some blue jeans carelessly thrown on the floor. Larry was right behind her, and as he jumped out of bed, he fell right on top of Jennie, knocking the wind out of her. To top everything off, his breath was a mixture of garlic and cigarettes.

They got up off the floor, and as they walked to the bathroom Jennie kicked aside shirts, blouses, panties, and three shoes. Only three shoes? Where was the other one? Why was the apartment always a pig sty? She figured she better clean it eventually. She pictured herself behind the wheel of a payloader with a huge bucket. She'd scrape up all the junk, and if Larry was in the way, she'd scoop him up, too. Then, as he was screaming, she would dump him onto a large pile of decaying garbage. Again she started giggling. By the time she explained to Larry about her "bucket" day dream, tears were streaming down her cheeks.

She really had the perfect life with no responsibility. She got drunk only on the weekends and smoked pot only five or six times a week. She had never finished high school, but she was fine. She had a great job as a waitress at the diner, and Larry really loved her. Her parents called him Scary Larry, but they didn't know him. Ten years ago, he had the coolest motorcycle, and he still owned it today. He made pretty good money driving a bread truck.

Jennie stumbled into the bathroom and flopped onto the seat. This room looked like it hadn't been cleaned since the building was first erected. What a mess. She wet her finger and wrote her name in the dirt on the floor. "That's really cool," she thought, "now everyone will know this is my apartment."

Jennie got into the shower and stood there for ten minutes. Her head was pounding, and every muscle in her body ached. Even the warm water did not relieve her cramps. She had scratches on her arms and chest. How had she gotten those marks? She couldn't wash her hair because she had forgotten to buy shampoo again. She made a feeble attempt to wash her body with the sliver of soap. Neither Jennie nor Larry cared about soap. It was a waste of time.

As she stood in the shower, she realized she had a song stuck in her head, and she couldn't stop it. "We Three Kings of Orient Are, La La La," she repeated over and over. She didn't know any of the other words and couldn't imagine why she was humming that song nonstop. Must be that was the final song she heard last night before she passed out. It was Christmastime.

When she got out of the shower, she toweled off with a T-shirt she picked up off the floor. Then, she looked on the floor for something clean to wear. The first thing she touched was the jeans from last night. They were covered with mud, not just on the backside from sitting in the mud behind the shack where they smoked their joints, but everywhere. They even had straw or grass stuck to them. She went to the pile of clothes on the floor of the closet and found some pants that didn't smell too bad and put those on.

As she was dressing, she wondered, "What happened last night anyway?" She remembered that she and Larry had run out of booze and the only thing open was the twenty-four hour Quick Mart. Larry's friend Chaz had a pickup truck, and they all crammed into the front seat for the drive there. At the store, they bought a case of beer and scored a little weed. Jennie remembered they went behind an old shack in a field, and drank and smoked. They were laughing uncontrollably about something, but for the life of her, she couldn't remember what.

Suddenly, she realized how hungry she was. She and Larry always slept until noon, at least. Now they would need to scrounge around in the kitchen to find something to eat. They always had bread because every day Larry copped a loaf or two from the truck. Jennie stood in front of the mirror and said to herself, "I want something awesome to happen today. I'd give anything if we had some excitement." She was bored out of her mind.

She was busy chewing a hangnail when she turned the corner into the kitchen and banged her shin on something big and hard. "What the . . . ?" She couldn't move. Right in front of her was an enormous baby Jesus. Jennie thought there is no way that this statue could fit through the door. "It's a Miracle. It's just what I asked for," she exclaimed.

She ran to the bedroom and got her cell phone, then quickly returned to the kitchen. She was almost positive the statue was just a hallucination and would not be there anymore. When she got to the kitchen, the Baby Jesus was still there. She took pictures of it from all angles, then immediately turned on her computer. Within seconds, she uploaded the pictures to her Facebook page. This magical gift just had to be shared with all her friends. After she wrote a short message, she turned to find Larry.

She saw him walking down the hall and grabbed his hand. "Hurry up. Look here. This mysteriously appeared in the kitchen," she said as they rounded the corner to the kitchen.

Larry stopped and put his arm around her. In a very condescending voice, he said, "You must be kidding. This didn't mysteriously appear, you dope. We stole it from that stupid manger after we got stoned."

Jennie just stood with her mouth open. "*Get out*. We stole it?" she screamed.

"Yeah. Way cool, ain't it?" Larry answered.

Larry went into a long explanation about trying to lift the statue into the back of the truck and uncontrollable laughing when they finally succeeded. It took about an hour for Chaz and the two of them to lug that thing up the stairs. They started to laugh again when they were trying to figure out how to get the statue in the door. Jennie even suggested that they coat the statue with Vaseline. Chaz finally dug a saw out of the back of his pick up and cut off part of the bottom of the statue.

Jennie sank onto the floor and stared at the Baby Jesus. Larry looked at her and realized her face was pure white. "What's wrong, babe?" he asked.

On the Edge

She didn't answer. She reached up and showed him the Facebook picture she had just posted. He stared at it for several minutes and said, "Bummer. Don't worry. Nobody reads your Facebook anyway."

That night she was feeling much better because none of her friends had written anything on her Facebook page. Maybe this whole thing would just blow over.

The next morning at ten, she was awakened from a drunken sleep. When she opened the door, two policemen stood in the hall with a warrant for her arrest. I guess some people really read Facebook.

She finally got the excitement she wanted. As they brought her out of the house in handcuffs, she was surprised to see reporters waiting for her. As the cameras were flashing, the only thought that came to her head was, "Paparazzi." Somehow she thought that was good, but suddenly the group surged forward and pressed on her and she felt smothered. Then the noise started:

"Jennie, Look this way."

"Jennie, I'm from Channel 20 in Fredericksburg. Why did you steal that statue from the Methodist Church?"

"Jennie, how did you lift that heavy statue? Who were you working with?"

"Jennie, whatever made you post the picture on Facebook? Didn't you know you would be caught?"

"Jennie, Jennie, Jennie," the screaming kept coming.

"Look here! Look here! Look here!"

§ § §

She was charged with grand larceny and was looking at five to ten years in jail. However, she got what she wished for—excitement. It only lasted two days and then the world moved on to another story.

Several months later, she heard from a friend that her name was on the list of "The Dumbest Crooks in the U.S.A." It was, after all, the first time her name appeared on any list of accomplishments. Jennie got a headache just thinking about it.

Samantha

Bobbie Troy

Why, Samantha? Why did you have to leave me? And without warning? I don't understand it. We had such a good and caring relationship. I thought it would last all our lives.

Dad, the vet just called. Someone found Samantha near his office and brought her in, but it was too late. The vet wants to know if you would like him to cremate Samantha. Dad, did you hear me?

Striptease Variation

Marlee Laws

Lili stared into her wine glass. She watched her problems drift away in the red liquid. In a dream-like stupor, she ignored her friends, let them carry on with their mindless chatter like they didn't know what they had to do. Curtain was in an hour. One more glass wouldn't hurt. They didn't notice.

Lili and the others sat tense in front of their mirrors. They applied masks of powder and ink, covering their faces in an invisible shield. One by one, the others finished, lips red and eyes large, they walked out onto the stage. She sat longer, despising the woman she saw in the mirror. She told herself that in just a few more minutes, a few more brush strokes, her face would belong to someone else. But today, like every other day, the familiar stranger she saw in the glass was only her.

Lili stepped out onto the stage. The curtain was closed, and the light shined dully through the folds. The others were in their places, sultry positions and lace teases, waiting for the show. She joined them, herself on display beneath the shear frills. With a creak, the curtain opened, swinging its heavy skirt to reveal the stage to prying eyes. She was blinded, there was a cheer, and the show began.

I Want To Be Human
Pennie Patterson

The view from this floor is really a bore.
Why can't I sit up in the chair
And smoke and drink coffee, watch big screen T.V.
Not from down here but up there?

When we go for a ride, I'm always confined
By the leash and the harness I hate.
If I could just drive, I know we'd arrive
Quite safely and never be late.

I could go to the pet store, not to the vet's door
Or visit my friends at the mall
And have a quick drink, a martini, I think,
Or maybe a beer, frosty and tall.

Dog food's okay but the same every day
And sometimes it gives me the heaves.
I'd like my own steak, some chocolate and cheesecake,
Not just what some human leaves.

Going out in the rain is a very big pain.
An indoor bathroom would be fine
And a nice steaming shower with adjustable power,
Like hers—I wish it were mine.

To do as I please would be such a breeze.
I'd not have to wait for her whim.
No pining away while she's gone all the day.
I could choose between home and the gym.

She sings those dumb songs about how she longs
To be a dog just like me.
Why this should be so, I really don't know.
A human's what I'd rather be.

Ba Da Bang!

Jack Daily

Miles Davis, the great jazz trumpeter, made the following statement about improvisation: "Play what you know and improvise above that."

Science may soon unwind the Big Bang to the instant of creation. As we close the first decade of the 21st century, discoveries made from NASA satellite data and scientists working across the many fields of physics have fueled a great debate. On one hand, you have the large-scale disciplines of astrophysics and cosmology. Physicists in those fields spend their days (and nights) with receding galaxies, dark matter, and dark energy, and talk over martinis about the event horizon of black holes. But these guys are at odds with their colleagues in the subatomic interrobang of particle physics. Nuclear physicists use words like quarks and mesons. Dinner-party talk gravitates toward the uncertainty principle and nuclear fusion. Nobody wants to see these guys throwing punches.

What happens next will more likely seem scripted by M. Night Shyamalan. As stated on Wikipedia, the Large Hadron Collider (LHC) is the world's highest-energy particle accelerator. It will be used to test the predictions of competing theories. The LHC accelerates opposing beams of particles around its seventeen-mile circular tube at near the speed of light. When these particles collide, all hell breaks loose.

The most important mission of the LHC is to prove the existence of the Higgs boson, or God particle, as described in the book by Nobel Prize-winning physicist Leon Lederman. The Higgs boson is the missing link that will unify today's disparate conclusions of large- and small-scale physics culminating in a *Theory of Everything*.

The highest energy experiment on this path of discovery is scheduled for December 2012. One concern is that the incredible energy necessary for this experiment could produce a microscopic black hole. Black holes exert so much gravitational pull that nearby objects rapidly fall into them, thereby increasing their size and power. The scientists at LHC believe that if a black hole were to be spawned by an LHC collision, it would be short-lived and unable to grow. If the math is flawed, it doesn't take much imagination to envision the other, apocalyptic outcome where continents and oceans become appetizers for an insatiable black hole followed by the solar system as entree.

In an unrelated field of study, the Mayan calendar predicts the end of the world on December 21, 2012.

So if you are reading this in 2013 or beyond, you can take satisfaction in knowing that the LHC calculations were correct, and the Mayan Calendar was not.

Postscript.

Ba Da Bang! was written in February 2012 during a creative writing workshop with a writers' prompt to "take something you know, then improvise". On July 4th 2012, scientists from the European Center for Nuclear Research (CERN) announced the discovery of the Higgs Boson, first postulated in 1964 by Scotsman Peter Higgs. It quickly became a media event labeled Higgs-Teria succinctly reported in a feature article of Time Magazine called Definite Particle by Jeffrey Kluger. But stay tuned. The LHC will continue to increase the energy of colliding particles until the end of 2013, or perhaps just the end.

Biographies

D.C. Ackerly is the penname of Dawn Latham who grew up on Long Island and Kansas. An enthusiastic traveler, Dawn has visited thirty-seven countries and lived for several years in England. Her work experience includes jobs in marketing, office administration, and publishing where she wrote for trade newsletters and catalogs. She now enjoys writing fiction, poetry, and short memoirs. Dawn is currently seeking representation for her first book, a middle-grade novel inspired by her son and his friends.

Isabelle Anctil was born and raised in the Greenfield area of western Massachusetts. She studied watercolor, print making, and collage with Nora S. Unwin an artist noted for wood carvings. Isabelle later moved to the west coast of Florida where she was a member of the West Pasco Art Guild for over twenty years. During that period, she served as an officer on the Board of Directors for the Art Guild and for five years chaired the annual Wild Life Art Show. She has completed many art workshops and classes, most notably with Larry Goldsmith and Roger Bamsemer. Her forte is extensively detailed colored pencil drawings. She is currently working in acrylics.

Arlene Baker has lived in Culpeper for twenty years. She was one of the original members of the Art Group and has remained a member for eighteen years. Her original artistic endeavors were with stained glass. Arlene has expanded her art work to include watercolor and acrylic paintings. She never had art instruction and considers her art self-taught. Most important, she enjoys the camaraderie of the artists and considers them her dear friends.

Jennifer Bierhuizen contributed writings to this publication.

Caryn Moya Block burst onto the paranormal romance scene with her debut e-book, *Alpha's Mate*, in January of 2012. Since then, she has published a second book, *A Siberian Werewolf in London*. She was named one of iReader Review's Top 50 Indie Authors for April 2012. She won the Global E-book Award in the Contemporary Romance category for 2012. Caryn is also one of the contributors to "Interviews with Indie Authors, Top Tips from Successful Self-Published Authors" by Claire and Tim Ridgeway. She lives with her husband of over thirty years and has two adult sons.

Dina Buckley grew up in rural northern Virginia and moved to Culpeper almost eighteen years ago. Some of her earliest memories included drawing horses. Dina studied the fundamentals of graphic design and animation at Northern Virginia Community College. She eventually earned an A.A.S. in Communication Design. Later employment led her down a path of technical documentation and software development. As her three children grew more independent, she found more time to devote to her creativity. While Dina likes all types of art, her favorite media are colored pencils and watercolor, and her favorite subject is still horses.

Diane Burdette grew up in New Jersey. She moved to Virginia in 1980 to teach elementary school. As an educator, she enjoyed reading stories to the students and teaching the writing process. While working for the school system, she was able to meet several authors who were visiting and spoke with them about writing children's literature. Since retiring two years ago, she has been focused on writing poetry, short stories, and books for young children.

Fran Cecere has a Master's Degree in Nursing and is originally from the Utica/Syracuse area. She has been living in Culpeper with her husband Roy Carter for nine years. In 2007 she joined the Pen-to-

Paper writers group and has been the facilitator for five years. The Windmore Foundation continues to be important to her, and she serves on the Board of Directors and functions as the Executive Director for the organization. In 2010 she helped edit *Images in Ink*, a collection of stories from Windmore writers. She enjoys incorporating fiction, humor, and real life events into her short stories. Her favorite subjects are her many grandchildren.

Cora DeJarnette Chlebnikow was born on Long Island in New York State. She studied writing at the University of Mary Washington and earned a MEd in reading education at the University of Virginia. Currently a pre-K - 5 literacy coordinator for the Madison County Public Schools, she is most proud of having taught in every school in Madison County, as well as in Charlottesville, Louisa, and Virginia Beach. Cora most enjoys writing poetry, though she also composes children's fiction and edits professionally. Cora has lived in Brightwood with her two daughters, her son, and her husband Jeff since 2001. She was first introduced to Windmore in 1995.

D.J. (Donna Jean) Christiano resides in Jeffersonton, Virginia, with her husband Tony and spirited Boston terrier, Sasha. She retired in 2008 after spending thirty-five years teaching in public schools. Writing stories about her family and childhood are her joys. She hopes that one day the stories will be entertaining to her grandchildren, Ryan and Sophia. Donna joined the Pen-to-Paper Writers group in January 2010 and found the group to be both inspiring and supportive. She plans to continue writing stories and plays for children of all ages.

Martha Orr Conn has been a resident of Culpeper for 25 years. She comes from a family of pilots, and her last book, *Crazy to Fly*, is a children's book about the early days of flying after World War I. It was a selection of the Junior Literary Guild. She enjoys writing humor, children's books, and how-to articles. She has sold a few short stories to magazines. One of her greatest achievements, she says, was to sell two stories to the *Virginia State Troopers Magazine* under the name, "Marty Conn," because it was a men's magazine that rarely accepted articles written by women.

Jack Daily, a native of Birmingham, Alabama, lives in Culpeper, Virginia. Most of his career was spent in Miami and the DC metropolitan area, supporting projects in the medical and space industry. Jack is an active member of the Alexandria Art League, the Windmore Foundation for the Arts, and belongs to Alabama's Eastern Shore Camera Club and Culpeper Photography Club. Jack is a bin artist in Alexandria's Torpedo Factory where he was selected in eleven of the Art League's juried shows during the 2010 and 2011 seasons. He was an author in Windmore's 2010 *Images and Ink* anthology and enjoys writing creative non-fiction, short stories, and poetry.

Judith Dreyer, MS, BSN, RN, adjunct lecturer, and public speaker, is a transplant to Virginia from Connecticut. She has degrees in nursing and nutrition and enjoys developing workshops and classes in a variety of holistic health topics. A Master Gardener, she contributes articles on wild edible and medicinal plants for several area newsletters. Pen-to-Paper gives her an opportunity to share poetry and short stories. You can visit her blog, *At the Garden's Gate*, by going to judithdreyer.com.

Herbert Frisbee worked for the federal government for many years, including a job in quality assurance with the Federal Aviation Administration. He started writing in his teens, but in 1995, after the death of his wife, he began writing in earnest. Although he composed short stories, he is best known for his humorous poetry, which was published in various magazines. Before Herb died in 2010, he expressed a wish to have his poetry continue to give pleasure to children and adults. His writing is presented to you with the permission of his family.

Martha Harris pursued her interest in art early in life. In the past few years, the farm she calls home in Orange County has given Martha inspiration for rural Virginia scenes and the surrounding Blue Ridge Mountains and mountain streams. These are typically painted in oil or acrylic. Flowers are also a favorite subject matter, and for these Martha prefers water colors. She continues to study technique and develop her skill. Her work is exhibited locally and has been added to many private collections.

John R. Henry, born on a farm in Jasper County, Mississippi, grew up to manage the family farm. He served in the Marine Corps during World War II. He graduated from Mississippi State University and worked as a technical writer for the U. S. Department of Agriculture. He has published his work in seventeen papers, eight magazines, two books, and five anthologies.

Bette Hileman is an independent writer, editor, and photographer. She retired in 2008 from a twenty-seven-year career writing and editing articles about the environment and health for the magazine *Chemical & Engineering News*. Currently, she is working on photography, short stories, and a novel. Many of her poems have been published in *vox poetica* and the blog-based journal *Orion Headless*. She co-edited two anthologies: *Images in Ink*, released in 2010 by Windmore Foundation for the Arts; and *Eclectic Brew*, released in 2011. In addition, she has edited five novels, including three by Caryn Block and one by Lavanda Woodall. She belongs to the cooperative gallery

Old Rag Photography in Sperryville, Virginia, and is listed in recent editions of Marquis' *Who's Who in the World* and *Who's Who in America*.

Sarah Calvert Hitt was a farmer's daughter, a farmer's sister, and a farmer's wife. She graduated from Mary Washington College and Columbia University. Sara worked in public education and as a vocational rehabilitation counselor. She was a life-long teacher of young children. In her retirement years, she resided at the Culpeper Baptist Retirement Community. She gave permission to use one of her stories in the 2012 anthology. She was pleased that people still appreciate her work. Sarah Calvert Hitt died on July 16, 2012.

Pennie L. Kinsey often writes under her Biblically-inspired penname Penniel Majenta. She resides in Culpeper, sharing space in late summer and early fall with occasional crickets that find her dwelling a welcome home. She is a member of Windmore and takes great joy in sharing her works with you.

Marlee Laws is a budding seventeen-year-old writer. She has been with the Pen-to-Paper writers group since she moved to Culpeper in 2007 and has composed an assortment of short stories, poems, and potential novels. Before coming to Culpeper, she lived in a variety of places as her father is a naval pilot. Last year, she spent the year abroad in Norway. For fun, she dabbles in music and various other artistic venues, but writing is where she finds the most enjoyment.

Sophi Link was born and raised in Madison County, Virginia. Sophi is a writer who prefers to work with poetry and non-fiction. The Virginia High School League awarded an honorable mention to her poem "Musical Memories" in 2010. Prior to graduation, she worked with the Windmore Foundation as an intern for her senior project.

Sophi attends the University of North Carolina at Asheville and is considering a degree in literature and language.

Gwen Monohan is a former teacher who has lived in Culpeper for nineteen years. Gwen had poems published in several journals over the years, including: *American Poets and Poetry, Blueline Anthology, Big Muddy, Cold Mountain Review,* and *Coe Review.* This past year she had a few poems published online at *vox poetica.* Several years ago she won first place in the Dover Beach Poetry Press competition for her poem, "Robin's Wake", and "Leavings" won an honorable mention and publication in *Second Wind.*

MaryAnn Morrison is a lifetime educator. Born in a small town on the Atlantic shore of New England in the middle of World War II, she was brought up to be patriotic, neighborly, humble, and resourceful. After raising her son, she moved to San Diego in 1989 and began her writing career as a poet for a gift-giving company. She missed education, so upon receiving her master's degree, she became a consultant for the Houghton Mifflin Company. This led to an opportunity to write her first non-fiction book, *WWII MAMpower,* the battle for gender equity as told by women who fought for it.

Nancy O'Connor was born in the mountains of Marion, North Carolina, but grew up in an apartment in Falls Church, Virginia. Nancy studied art in high school and at Madison College and has experience in ceramics, drawing, acrylic, collage, and most recently watercolors. Most of her recent art experience has been through art classes, workshops, and self-study. Her paintings include old barns, old beach houses, lighthouses and other outdoor scenes. She lives in Madison County, Virginia, and is active in the Windmore Foundation of the Arts in Culpeper.

Pennie Patterson was born in Newark, New Jersey, but shortly after, her family moved to Florida. She attended Emory University. Pennie continued her education by studying music at Moravian College and the University of Tennessee. Since her teens, she has been writing historical novels, poetry, and comic or cosmic romantic stories. She loves horses and has taught horseback riding and published articles in the Clifton Horse Society newsletter. In recent years, she has been writing poems and short stories, as well as novels about Indian life, space romance, and murder.

Carol Pivarnik is a watercolor artist who specializes in dogs. Her book, *Doggitude*, published the fall of 2012, features thirty-six of her expressive dog portraits, accompanied by humorous "dog-think" haiku. Carol works at her Brindle Studio in Castleton, Virginia.

Lois Griffin Powell is from Milford, Connecticut. She attended Hampton University and graduated from Southern Connecticut State University. Lois received her Master's Degree in Writing and taught writing in Babylon, Long Island. Four of her poems have been published in poetry anthologies. She has written articles for local papers and loves writing children's stories and poems. Lois and her husband moved to Lake of the Woods in Locust Grove, Virginia, in 2003. They have two sons, one daughter, and five grandchildren. She has recently joined Windmore and hopes to get more involved with the organization.

Ruby E. Pruitt and her family moved to the Culpeper area in 2009. She joined Windmore's Pen-to-Paper writing group in 2011. Ruby has written poetry since elementary school and wrote her first poem in second grade. Two local places she occasionally shares her talents are Our Father's House retirement home and The Ravens Nest Coffee House. Her song, "Praise the Lord Anyway" won the Nokesville

"Idol" competition in 2003. Ruby does not take her gifts of singing and writing lightly. She has written Bible stories, poetry, songs, and is also working on a craft book.

Lisa Pugh was born in Illinois and has been writing fiction since she was nine. She composes romance, historical fiction, and science fiction. She earned an English degree in 1995 from Hollins University and a Master's in Library and Information Science in 1997 from Louisiana State University. She has lived in Texas, Louisiana, the United Kingdom, Maryland, and Virginia. She moved to the Culpeper area in 2007 and now lives in Boston, Virginia with her husband, young daughter and dog.

Nancy Scott was born in southern Illinois. She attended Northwestern University as a drama student. She has been writing, publishing, and giving readings of her poetry for many years. She currently resides in Virginia with her husband Scott and her cat Goldie.

Jan Settle is the owner and director of Jan Settle Design Studios. As a child growing up in Culpeper, Virginia, she frequented art shows and meetings with her mother, a member of the original group of local artists who became the Artists of Windmore. She joined Windmore Foundation for the Arts in 2006. In addition to painting, she has tried writing. She lives with her husband Ricky in Castleton, Virginia, at the foot of the beautiful Blue Ridge Mountains in a home they designed together.

Cynthia Siira was born in St. Cloud, Minnesota. Her father's job with the State Department took the family to Africa when she was five. She lived in Libya, Somalia, and Ethiopia and graduated from the American Community School in Addis Ababa, Ethiopia. She returned to the States and has made Culpeper her home for the past twenty-two years. Cynthia has always enjoyed writing and has finished a book on her family's experiences in Libya. Other books are in various stages of completion, including a mystery and juvenile fiction.

Jeanne Tanks was nine-months old when a fever severely impaired her vision. She remained legally blind until the problem was identified and corrected when she turned fourteen. Jeanne earned a Bachelor's Degree in Studio Art from the University of Mary Washington, studied art in Europe and the United States, and took graduate classes and independent studies in glassmaking. Jeanne has mastered a myriad of art media, including: oil, encaustic, and silk painting; stone and precious metal sculpting; paper and printmaking; photography, Photoshop, and digital art; ceramic art; and advanced kiln-formed glass art. In recent years, Jeanne has pioneered several new techniques for producing world-class works of art, using warm glass as a 2-D format.

Bobbie Troy maintains her sanity and perspective on life by writing flash fiction, poetry, and original fairy tales with a 21st century twist. Her work appears in many online and print journals. A few are *vox poetica, SPARK, Caper Literary Journal, Leaf Garden Press, Yes, Poetry, Cavalcade of Stars, The Journal of Microliterature,* and *The Camel Saloon*. Her poem "Dear Diane", was nominated for a 2010 Pushcart Prize. Her fairy-tale play, *Sasha and the Tree of Sorrows*, was produced in March 2011. Bobbie also served on the editorial board for *Saltian*, a collection of poems by Alice Shapiro.

Kathy Webber contributed illustrations to this publication.

Kathleen Willingham lives in southern Fauquier County with her husband Carl, daughter Sarah, and old dog Cody. Kathleen retired after forty years as an art teacher in Fauquier County. She is a member of Brush Strokes Gallery in Fredericksburg, River District Arts in Sperryville, Windmore Artists group, and an associate member of the Lorton Workhouse. She also participates in the Fredericksburg Center for the Creative Arts where she is a docent and an editor of their newsletter. Kathleen enjoys working in pastel and oil and often paints plein-air landscapes using these media. She has created series of paintings that relate to or evolve from themes or abstract concepts.

Lavanda Woodall, humorist, storyteller, and short-story author, is a Korean War veteran and mother of five. Her stories about Cade County and its county seat of Cades Ridge have a ring of truth, while bringing a chuckle to the reader. These imaginary pieces are possibly set in northeast Georgia, southeast Tennessee, or southwest North Carolina, depending on what day of the week it is. The narrator of Lavanda's stories is an unmarried lady in her sixties, who is kin to most of the Cade County folk—and knows the rest of them very well. Her intentional misuse of the English language adds to the humor in her down-home stories. In addition, Lavanda has e-published her first romance novel, *The Rancher and His Lady*.

jd young, a displaced Bronx native, resides in Virginia with her husband. She has published two books, *Scarlett's Letters* and *The Butter Pecan Diaries,* that are filled with laughter and wry humor. Both have five-star reviews on Amazon. She believes the place where she lives, a remote and heavily wooded haven with moonlight shadows and bumps in the night, fuels her imagination to run the gamut from ordinary, to fearful, to bizarre. Her latest offerings open the door to reveal her intense and oftentimes dark view of life.